Two Monog

After the Hurricane:

The Misadventures of Quincy Carter

A Novel by S. R. Graham

Cover Designed by S. R. Graham

Hello, readers!

This is After the Hurricane: The Misadventures of Quincy Carter, book 6 of the *Two Monogamous* Series. If you have not read book 1, *Two Monogamous,* book 2, *I Call It Karma,* and book 3, *Drown the Lovers,* book 4, *Face Off,* and book 5, *Who Do You Love? Jarrah's Choice,* you will not fully understand what's going on in this book, since it continues where the fifth book left off.

This book also addresses mental health issues, sexual harassment, violence and abuse, alcoholism, and death, which could serve as triggers to readers. It contains sexually explicit and vulgar language. So, if any of these things might offend you, I suggest that you don't read it. Also, I did extensive research on the information I included in the book, but I am not a professional researcher so there could be some inaccuracies. I ask that you not condemn me for that.

Thank you for purchasing and/or downloading this book! If you are okay with the previously mentioned warning, I hope you enjoy the shift in storyline as you get to know Quincy through his eyes. He finally let's Jarrah go and tries to explore romance with two other women. However, the drama doesn't stop for him, causing him to get more than he bargained for. This is book one of a three-part series for The Carter Brothers (Quincy and Marcus). I decided to give them a mini-series to give you all their backstory. It was so difficult to write from the perspective of a narcissist, so I hope I did Quincy justice. Happy reading!

Love,

S. R. Graham

Table of Contents

Prologue: Love Ain't Enough

September 17, 2015
Fulton County Courthouse
Atlanta, Georgia

Watching Jarrah walk away from me as I stood in front of Fulton County Courthouse was the hardest thing I'd done in my life. Everything inside of me was telling me I made the biggest mistake of my life, but I was bound by my ego and pride. Plus, I could see in her eyes she was barely holding it together, and I didn't want to make her suffer more than I already had. I may have been too much of an asshole to say it out loud, but I dropped the ball when it came to my relationship with her. However, I couldn't deny that a part of me felt like I could get her back when I wanted to. I was her first everything like she was mine, so I couldn't see her being with anyone other than me. It may have been cocky of me to assume that, but regardless of the state of our relationship, and the distance she moved away from me, she would always be my wife. I was certain there was no one in this world who could take my place. Jarrah loved me even more than she loved herself, so no matter where she went or who she was with, I would always be the one for her.

When I first met Jarrah as a kid, I knew immediately that she would be my forever. It may have taken her a little while to see me that way, but I felt it in my spirit she would always be in my life. She was loyal to a fault. With everything I took her through, she still looked at me with those piercing hazel eyes like I was heaven on earth for her. Nothing I did changed the way she treated me, and I'd be the first to admit I took her love for granted. She stuck by me through everything, so I knew the hold I had on her heart. I cheated, lied, gambled away our savings, mistreated her, and manipulated her into blaming herself for it all. However, she still loved and cared about me like she did when we first met. Although she was walking away from me, I was the one who asked for the divorce, so that meant I had the power. Seeing her leave for Chicago hurt me a little, but I knew all I had to do was apologize for what I did, and ask her to come back to me, and she would. However, I was a free man, so I could do whatever the fuck I wanted to without guilt hanging over my head.

Once Jarrah was gone, I walked over to my new all black 2015 Lincoln MKX, and got in. I bought it as a gift for myself for my divorce. I had been wanting a new car for a while, but I held off on it since Jarrah and I had been trying to get pregnant. There was nothing I wanted more than to be a father to Jarrah's kids, so I was so disappointed she could never get pregnant for me. It made me view her differently, which in turn made me feel like she wasn't for me.

That was the sole reason I wanted to divorce her since aside from that, she was the perfect wife. Regardless of that though, no woman would ever come close to Jarrah in my mind. I just had a tough time accepting we would never have kids together. So, I guess my purpose for letting her go was more for me to see if there were better out there for me. I couldn't give a woman my all while still married to her, so I didn't have a choice but to leave her. I was prepared to go back on my hands and knees if I couldn't find what I was looking for though. Since I was officially back on the market, I felt like I needed a new toy to attract the ladies to me. Jarrah may have made me take a blow to my pockets by getting half of my money in the divorce, but I was still going to stunt if I wanted to. My net worth wasn't twenty-five million anymore, but I was still a rich man, especially by Atlanta's standards, so that made me an eligible bachelor. I turned up my radio, and blasted J. Holiday's song, Forever Ain't Enough on repeat as I made my way to my hotel in downtown Atlanta.

When I got to The Carter on Luckie Street Northwest, I pulled up to the front, and quickly hopped out. Then, I hooped my keys to my valet, so he could park my car in my parking spot. I had a meeting with some potential partners, and I was running late. As I rushed to the conference room of my hotel, I threw my black Givenchy blazer on, and buttoned it up, so I could look presentable. It was hard for me to get a meeting with them, so the last thing I wanted to do was blow my chance. The hospitality business was oversaturated already, so I couldn't afford to give them an opportunity to make a deal with someone else. I was still new to the industry, so it wasn't like I had built an undisputed reputation yet. I wasn't as well-known as I aspired to be, so I knew I only had one time to fuck up before rumors spread that I was a bad businessman. Jarrah and I worked hard to build this empire, and now I had to keep things afloat without her. That was going to be the hardest thing about her not being my wife anymore, especially since she moved to Chicago. I knew she only moved because she didn't feel like she would be strong enough to deny me any help I needed from her. So, I had to do this shit myself.

As I was about to enter the conference room, my potential partner was on their way out the door. My assistant immediately shot me a look that suggested I fucked up. I stood in the doorway to block their path, so I could explain myself. "Mr. Patel, I apologize for getting here so late. I had some important business to take care of that couldn't wait," I explained. He sighed deeply as he tapped his feet on the marble floors.

"Mr. Carter, I am a busy man. I don't have time to waste with you. I have plenty of people who want to do business with me that value my time. You should be thankful I bothered to show up," he chastised through thin lips as he ran his fingers through his coarse straight chestnut brown hair. He favored the Hindi film actor Shah Rukh Khan with his wide sharp nose, honey brown eyes, and hooded brows that made him look like he didn't take any bullshit, but at his core, he was a kind man. He just didn't play when it came to business, which was what I admired about him.

"I understand, Mr. Patel. There's no excuse for why I wasn't here on time. It's just that I was going through a divorce with my now ex-wife, and I had to show up to court today. I just need a few minutes of your time. I promise it won't be a waste," I convinced. He hesitated a bit, so he could ponder what I was asking him. I held my breath and prayed he agreed to give me a second chance.

"I have a few meetings set up after this, but... I will have my assistant call you to reschedule our meeting for next week. That's the best I can do for you, Mr. Carter," he told me. I smiled and held out my hand for him to shake. I wanted to talk to him as soon as possible, but I knew I didn't have a choice but to wait until next week.

"Thank you so much, Mr. Patel! I promise you won't regret it," I assured him. He nodded his head at me and left the hotel with his employees following him like ducklings. I walked into the conference room, and sat in my seat, and let all the air out of my body. I was relieved I had another chance to pitch my idea to him. I was trying to elevate my business, so I could gain the recognition, status, and money I always dreamed of as a little boy. Jarrah may not have been around to be my crutch, but I still had the burning desire and ambition to be successful.

"That was a close call," my assistant Kiandra said as she closed the door, locked it, and made her way back over to me. My eyes scanned her slim, curvy, fit body as she walked behind my chair. She began massaging my back as I closed my eyes and relished her tender touch. I hadn't had sex since we started going to court for the divorce because I didn't want to slip up and give Jarrah the leverage, she needed to take me for everything I had. Half was too damn much if you asked me, so I stayed away from other women just in case she had someone watching me. She signed a prenup in the beginning of our marriage that stated she was entitled to half of what we made together, and if she could prove I was cheating on her, she could get seventy percent of what I was worth. Jarrah wasn't spiteful or greedy, so I wasn't worried about her going to those lengths, but I held out just to be sure. She didn't care about my money. However, her lawyer took it upon herself to hit me as hard as she did, and even though I was angry at first, I knew she deserved it all. I fucked around on her since before we even got married, so holding out for those last few months was the least I could do.

"You feel tense," Kiandra told me as she kneaded the tension from my shoulders. She was turning me on. I tried to control my urges because she was nothing but a tease. I had been wanting to take it there with her, but she'd only let it go so far before she stopped it. I tried to just focus on my plans for this hotel, but it was hard. She had the skills of a real masseuse to say she was an assistant.

"So, how did things go in court? Is the divorce final," she asked me.

"Aside from her getting half of my money, things went well. As of today, I'm officially a single man," I confirmed. Her movement halted for a few seconds, causing me to open my eyes abruptly.

"Good," she said. Then, she slid my chair away from the table, and straddled me. That's when I noticed she took off her dress. All she was wearing was a black bra and boy short panties with her black strappy six-inch heels. She was sexy as fuck. She wasn't as thick as my wife, but she had nice sized, tear drop shaped breasts that I usually couldn't keep my eyes off of when she was around. Her whole body was toned right, and she had nice thick thighs, and a firm curvy butt. I could tell she was a gym rat by her shape. My hand went directly to her ass like it had a mind of its own and rested there for a while. I had wanted Kiandra since the day I hired her, but I didn't want to make the first move since it would have been inappropriate.

"I've been craving you all of this time, but I didn't want to cross the line out of respect for your wife. Plus, you're my boss… but, if it's okay with you, I'd like to make those fantasies come true that you've been having about me from the day I walked in the door," she admitted. I stared at her pretty pink demanding lips. It was like they were begging me to give them some attention, so I closed my eyes and slowly leaned in for a kiss. Her lips were as soft and delectable as I imagined. Her sweet scent invaded my nostrils as I fed on her lusciousness and made my dick shapeshift into metal. Just like that, she had my undivided attention. Suddenly, my thoughts about Jarrah and my business with Mr. Patel were long gone.

"Mmm, you taste so good, Quincy," she whispered into my mouth. I bit into my bottom lip and looked into her deep brown mesmerizing eyes as I caressed her ass cheeks. Her skin was so smooth and silky that I couldn't keep my hands still.

"Oh yeah? I got something that'll give you cavities," I retorted, before kissing the side of her mouth. Then, I pressed my erection into her thigh as we held eye contact. She smirked at me. Then, she got off me, and dropped down to her knees. She carefully undid my pants as she entranced me in her dreamy eyes. I bit my lip and waited anxiously for her to suck me off. It had been a while since I had sex. Kiandra was fine as hell too. I dreamed of fucking her for so long my dick throbbed anxiously as I waited on her next move. When she pulled my hard dick out my pants, she eyed it for a while with a smile on her face. I didn't have the biggest dick, but I was above average. However, I could tell she was satisfied with what I was working with.

Kiandra eased her mouth on my dick. I closed my eyes briefly to process what was happening. I may have been a cheater, but this was the first time I had sex with an employee of mine. I was attracted to Kiandra in every way, but I exercised self-control around her unless she made a move on me. She never allowed things to go this far with me, so I was in a state of shock at her actions. Kiandra tongued the head of my dick as she mesmerized me. I looked down at her, before giving her a scalp massage since her hair was too curly for my fingers to get through. I closed my eyes and expelled warm air as she slowly swallowed my dick, taking a little of it in her mouth at a time until the whole thing disappeared. The euphoria coursing through my body made my toes curl inside my shoes. She sucked in her cheeks and jaw and bobbed her head on me with swift meticulous motions. I was a preemie, but I fought hard to hold my nut. I loved the visual of her taking all of me in her mouth. It made me feel powerful. There was something about having a woman on her knees bowing to me that made me feel like a man. Kiandra quickly slid her mouth off my dick, making a popping sound that echoed off the walls in the conference room. Then, she slapped it against her tongue as I followed her every move while she put on a freak show. She spat on my shaft and continued deep throating me while stroking my dick like she was wringing out a wet rag.

"Aaaah shit," I groaned as I came hard. She sucked my sperm out of me like my dick was a Capri sun. It was sexy as hell to me. When my fluids were in her stomach, she straddled me again. I spanked her ass cheeks to thank her. Finally, I was going to have her like I wanted her.

"I've been thinking about this for so long, Q. I just hope it doesn't interfere with our work environment," she expressed to me. There was a speck of hesitance in her dark eyes, so I knew I needed to validate her feelings, but I had a one-track mind. I began massaging her clit through her lace boy short panties.

"I've wanted your fine ass for so long. Get wet for me so I can put this dick in you," I commanded. She sandwiched her bottom lip between her teeth as she peered at me through desperate moon eyes. I could tell we were on the same page. When her pussy was salivating and I had on a condom, I pulled her panties to the side, lifted her up, and sat her on my dick.

"Fuck," I mumbled as her pussy enclosed my dick. It felt warm and cozy like a heated blanket. This was my first-time having sex with her, so I wanted to make a good impression. I didn't want this to be the last time I got to experience her. First, she slowly rode my dick. Then, she gradually sped up her pace after the first two minutes. I held onto her waist as I assisted her and sucked on her breasts and nipples.

"Mmmm, Quincy. You feel so good baby," she whined. I held her tight and plowed into her. Both of our chests heaved as the sexual energy ran through us.

"Oooo," Kiandra moaned as she released. I could feel myself about to climax too, so I abruptly lifted her off my dick, picked her up, and bent her over on the table. Then, I inserted my rigid dick back inside her and deep stroked her as I held her by the arms. I stirred my dick in her thoroughly as I enjoyed watching her juicy lip-shaped ass from the back.

"Aaaah, I'm about to cum. I'm about to cum all over your dick," she warned me before her body jerked. After that, I was comfortable enough to let loose, so I did. When I was done, I carefully slid my condom off, and headed into the bathroom to dump it. I had been adamant about not getting anyone other than Jarrah pregnant, so I always used condoms, and I always disposed of them myself. I refused to be trapped by any woman. I knew Jarrah wasn't with me anymore, but until I found someone worth replacing her, I still only wanted a family with her.

After I cleaned myself up, I walked back into the conference room with Kiandra, and said, "Get back to work." Then, I left, and headed to my office.

I may have wanted to experience Kiandra since I hired her, but I wasn't interested in having anything serious with her. I could tell she was the relationship type. The fact that she waited until I got my divorce told it all. I may have been an asshole, but I always made it known how I wanted things to go when I was involved with someone, whether it was in a committed relationship or a friend with benefits situation. No matter how much they tried, none of the women I'd dealt with measured up to Jarrah. We may not be together anymore, but she would always be the one I want to have my babies. However, since she couldn't I felt like I owed it to myself to see what else was out there. As much as I loved Jarrah, love wasn't enough. I wanted a family too. I was stuck between a rock in a hard place, not knowing if I made the right decision or not, but since I was a free man, I'd find out soon enough.

Prologue 2: The Grass Ain't Greener

September 19, 2016
Highland Square Apartment Complex
Atlanta, Georgia

The sunlight peeking through the blinds in my master bedroom acted as an alarm for me. I slowly opened my eyes and looked toward the clock on my nightstand. It was six 'o' clock in the morning, and I was already awake. I usually awoke at seven, but my sleep schedule had been thrown all the way off in the past year. I habitually looked over to Jarrah's side of the bed and felt a longing feeling in the pit of my stomach. There had been a void I'd been desperately trying to fill after she left. I knew I made a big mistake divorcing her immediately after the divorce was final, but it was my decision, so I had to deal with the consequences. So much had happened in a year, and I had been in a funk for the past few weeks. I thought the bachelor life was going to give me the clarity I needed to move forward with my life with or without Jarrah, but all I gained was more debt, problems, and the pressure of failure. My hotels had gone under since Jarrah left because I was bad with my money. I lost the deal I had with Mr. Patel, I ran through half of my money trying to cover my ass, and I was facing a sexual harassment complaint because I refused to give Kiandra the commitment, she wanted from me.

Women could be vindictive as hell when they didn't get their way. I knew I shouldn't have mixed business with pleasure, but I let my hormones dig this hole for me, so I had to stand in it.

Kiandra knew as well as I knew that I never sexually harassed her. After my divorce, she had been throwing that Jamaican pussy at me every day. I even caught her digging in the trashcan for the condoms we had been using, but I wasn't stupid enough to leave them where she could get them. I always dumped them in the dumpster outside the hotel so she wouldn't have access to my seed, but since she couldn't trap me, she decided to report me for sexual harassment. I shook my head and slid my hand down my face as I thought about all the shit I had gotten into. It was safe to say I had completely fucked up my life since Jarrah left. When she was here, she kept me in check. She always had my back, so I never had to worry about a thing. I took advantage of that back then. Now, I was filled with so much regret. As soon as she couldn't give me something I wanted I casted her aside like she meant nothing to me. It was fucked up, but I didn't know how to change my behavior. I was so used to her coming through for me that I couldn't handle it when she couldn't, and I knew it was unfair to her. I missed her so much I hired a private investigator to check on her in Chicago. I wanted to know what she was up to since she left me. So far, she was doing well for herself in her career, but when he called me yesterday to tell me he followed a guy to her condo, I started to feel uneasy.

I allowed Jarrah to move to Chicago because I believed she would always be mine. I was her first love and the one who took her virginity. She hadn't had sex with anyone else and I never thought she would. However, a guy going to her condo after midnight meant one thing, and that was something I couldn't handle. I threw my cover off me and sat up on the side of my bed. I exhaled deeply and stared into space. Ever since I was a little boy, I hated myself. I never thought I was anything special. My mother cared more about my father, alcohol, and drugs more than she cared about me, and my father was no longer with us. I wasn't the most athletic or popular kid. I was bullied in school because my mother didn't care enough to buy me decent clothes to wear, so I had to wear the same four outfits all of the time. We couldn't afford the nice shoes and name brand clothes that my peers would wear, so I had to wear tennis shoes from Walmart. Until I met the hazel eyed little girl with the big afro when I was seven years old, I was a nobody. Jarrah and Mama Charmaine were the only people who actually loved me. I didn't have many real friends and my family wasn't worth shit. The only way I could get through my shitty life was to armor myself with arrogance, indifference, and selfishness. Adopting this asshole persona was how I protected myself from getting hurt.

With Jarrah, I didn't have to dress myself in armor, and if I were being honest, that's what made me fall in love with her in the first place. I fucked up big time when I allowed her to go to Chicago. My ego influenced me to believe she would never betray me by being with someone else, especially in that way. I stood up and walked to my bathroom, so I could take a piss. It was Sunday morning, so I wasn't in a rush since I had nowhere to go. I had been in a bad mood for months after having to file bankruptcy for my business. Jarrah and I worked our asses off getting those hotels off the ground, and within a year, I fucked it all up. I wasn't completely broke yet. I had just enough to pay the loans off. The bank had been on my ass about their money, so I worked something out with them that allowed me six months to pay them back or they would seize my businesses. I had about six million left in my accounts, but all of that money was spoken for. I just let it sit in there because I didn't have it in me to give all of my money away. I knew it would take care of my debt to the bank, and to the crooked bookies I gambled with, but I had a crippling fear of being broke. I figured hiding out in my apartment was better than giving everything up.

While I brushed my teeth, I looked at myself in the mirror, and couldn't recognize who I was anymore. I had gotten so obsessed with wealth, status, and making a name for myself that I dug myself in a grave. The only person who gave a fuck about me left me, so I was left alone to deal with my own bullshit for once and it was uncomfortable. When I was done washing up, I left the bathroom, and went back to my bed. I picked up my cell phone to check my notifications since I had my ringer turned off. I was tired of getting phone calls from everyone looking for the money I owed them, so I decided to ignore them. I knew it was dangerous since some of the people I owed were mobsters who didn't mind pulling up on me and taking my life if I didn't pay them back. It happened to me so many times in the past, I no longer cared. Jarrah worked overtime to rectify the situations when they happened, but I didn't have her anymore. I guess I just had to be okay with losing my life. As if on cue, I got a call from the private investigator I hired. I immediately answered the phone.

"Hello," I exhaled as I pressed the warm phone into my right ear.

"What's up man? I was calling to give you an update on your wife," he announced. I sighed silently and braced myself for the news.

"What about her," I hesitantly asked. He paused for a few seconds, making my stomach rumble.

"The guy that went to her condo last night didn't leave until this morning. I followed him to an architecture company called The Vargas Brothers Architecture Company. I did a search on them, and it seems like they're a big deal, not just in Chicago, but in the country. They're loaded, no kids, no previous wives, or anything like that. They seem like clean cut guys. If she's starting a relationship with one of them, you're in trouble… If it were me, I would get on the next thing smoking to Chicago and get my wife back before it was too late," he advised. I sucked my teeth. Jarrah may have been interested in one of them, but she didn't care about money and material things.

"Thanks man. Stay on them for the next few days until I figure things out here," I told him.

"I gotchu. I hope things work out for you man. I know how it is to lose to guys like them. I lost my wife a long time ago in a comparable situation. Prepare yourself for what's to come," he stated. I nodded my head like he could see me. I heard what he was saying, but a part of me still felt like Jarrah would always be mine.

"Aight man. I'll be in touch," I said to him. He was a PI, not a therapist. I wasn't interested in talking to him about my problems. I was already in my feelings about everything I was dealing with. I didn't want to wallow in my pity for too long, so I dialed the number of the person who always told me what I needed to hear to get back on track.

"Q! Hey, son. How are you on this bright Sunday morning," Mama Charmaine cheerfully questioned. I instantly smiled at the sound of a smile in her voice. I could tell she was in a good mood.

"Hey Ma. I'm doing okay, I guess. How are you," I responded.

"I'm okay. Not feeling the best today, so I won't be making it to the Sunday service this morning. I thank God for life though," she answered. Hearing she wasn't feeling well alarmed me a little since that was rare.

"What's wrong? You need me to come over and take you to the emergency room," I asked her all at once. Her breath bounced off the speaker of the phone as she exhaled.

"No, I'm good, Q. I think I just need to rest."

"You sure," I pushed. It wasn't like I was doing anything else, and I could use the time together with her. I wasn't the best son lately because I was dealing with my own shit. I needed to make up for that somehow.

"Yes, son. I'm sure. What are you up to today," she inquired. I sat quietly for a few seconds. I didn't want her to know what was going on with me, but I wanted her to assure me that things would be okay.

"Nothing much, Mama. Just relaxing today," I lied. I rubbed my hand down the side of my face out of frustration. I couldn't believe all that happened in a year's time. It was like I was jinxed or something.

"Mmmhm. You sure everything's okay? You don't sound like yourself," she pointed out. I shook my head at her for calling me out.

"Everything's cool, Ma. Just one of those days," I replied.

"Well, you know you can talk to me about anything. I know the divorce been hard on you too, even though you don't like to admit it," she retorted. All I could focus on was the hint she dropped about Jarrah struggling too.

"Too? Have you spoken to Jarrah lately," I asked her, ignoring everything else she said.

"It's been a few days since I last spoke to her, but… of course she's having a hard time, Quincy. She didn't want to end things with you."

I sighed loudly and shook my head, before saying, "I know. I know. I did this to us."

"That's true, but it's okay to admit you havin' a tough time, son. You love Jarrah and you have been with her since you were seven years old. That's a hard habit to break."

"You're right. I thought I was doing the best thing for both of us," I acknowledged as I palmed my forehead.

"Well, did you find the answers you were looking for," she questioned. I chuckled under my breath. Of course, Mama would read me like a book. She may not have given birth to me, but she was my mother. I was an idiot, but I respected her more than I respected my own mother. Shit, I didn't even fuck with my mother like that. That's why I had such an issue with women.

"All I did was ruin my life. I guess this is what I get for treating Jarrah the way I did. She always deserved better from me after everything she's done for me," I admitted. I could hear Mama Charmaine snicker through the phone.

"You're right about that one," she joked. I chuckled.

"But… you know you aren't worthless, Q. That's the one thing both Jarrah and I wanted to make sure you knew. You sell yourself short and do yourself a disservice when you cheat yourself out of life because you don't think you deserve more. I love you like you my blood son, Quincy. I saw so much potential in you at an early age. Why do you think I took you in? I knew you just needed people to love and believe in you. Although you aren't with my daughter anymore, you're still my son. You were my son before you became my son-in-law. Don't ever forget the family you have. You don't have to go through things alone. You've worked hard to get to where you are. You gotta do everything in your power to get that all back," she stated. My eyes widened.

"Mama how did you know I lost everything?"

"Please, Q. I know everything. I am your mother," she stated. I smiled. I was proud to be her son.

"I promise, Ma. I'm going to do everything I can to get everything back," I declared as I walked over to the mirror and stared at my reflection. I made that promise to her, but it was mostly for myself. I had to bounce back from this. There was no other choice. My life had been perfect before I let Jarrah go. Our relationship wasn't perfect, but she was the perfect wife. I had been the one with the issues and she loved me still. Why couldn't I have held onto my love for her when she couldn't get pregnant for me? What I did was so fucked up. Jarrah didn't deserve it at all, but I was going to show her I was sorry, and I wanted my life with her back.

"Do what you have to do, Quincy, but don't go disrupt Jarrah's peace just because things aren't working out for you right now. I've forgiven you for hurting her countless times in the past, but I won't forgive you if you do it again. Do I make myself clear," she asked me, taking me back to my childhood. I stood and watched myself in silence for a while. Then, I nodded my head at my reflection.

"Yes ma'am," I responded. The man I was looking at didn't deserve Jarrah, but I was willing to become better for her. It wasn't hard for me to recognize I needed her. It was because of her that I got as far as I did. She sacrificed everything to help me, so I knew I had to do the same if I wanted her back. After she left me, things just fell apart. It was like her absence created a domino effect of bad luck. I thought of all the things I lost in the past year. My hotels were in jeopardy of being seized, my money was basically gone, and I had a sexual harassment complaint filed against me to human resources. However, I needed to put those things behind me and focus on getting my wife back. The only way I would get my perfect life back is if I got my perfect wife back. Regardless of what I had to do. I was coming back to Atlanta with Jarrah by my side where she belonged.

Chapter 1: A Heart's Surrender

February 10, 2017
Highland Square Apartment Complex
Atlanta, Georgia

When Donald and I left the grocery store with our hostage, we returned to my apartment complex in Atlanta. We could have gone after Jarrah and easily took her from those weird ass twins, but a part of me wanted to see if she would willingly choose me over them. I was her husband, and she only knew them for a few months, so I should have been her priority. I knew I caused her nothing but trouble and pain over the last few years, but everything I did was misguided. I loved Jarrah, but it was hard for me to accept that she couldn't give me the kids I desperately wanted. She was my wife, and she was supposed to be by my side forever. So, instead of forcing her to be with me, I took Mama Charmaine's replacement as leverage. I knew the only way they would take me seriously was if I took drastic measures. Besides, I was tired of sending other people to do my dirty work. I went to great lengths to stay under the radar so they wouldn't know I was still alive. That's how I was able to wreak havoc on their lives like I did. The last piece on the chess board was the queen, and it was up to her to make her move.

Being without Jarrah all of this time drove me crazy. I planned to go to Chicago to wine and dine her and get her to get on the plane with me so we could come back home to Atlanta. However, I had to watch her have the life I wanted with her with those niggas, and it broke me. When I found out she was pregnant for Dario, I nearly lost my entire mind. It made me feel like I had been the reason she couldn't get pregnant, which was a huge blow to my ego. Then, to find out she got pregnant again after her miscarriage was a slap in the face. Those twins must have had super sperm. Truthfully, I was jealous as hell they could get her pregnant so easily when I had been trying since we got married. That shit was hard to accept. It was like God was telling me I didn't deserve to share something so precious with her. I didn't want that to be our truth, so I held onto hope that she would grow tired of going through so much with them and choose me. Our life before this was simple, so I knew she was tired of all the plots and schemes. That's why I came here. I knew she would come back home after she had enough of the drama. Being right gave me hope she was ready to be my wife again. Although the baby she was carrying wasn't mine, I was willing to pretend it was if it meant I would have her back in my life. I was that desperate.

Almost losing my life made me realize the only good thing about my life was Jarrah. I was nothing without her. That was apparent to me when I lost everything after she left. I came to Chicago thinking this was going to be an easy feat. I never expected things to get so out of hand. I met Isabelle by chance, but she seemed to have been familiar with me from the beginning, so maybe meeting me was a part of her plan. I always wondered how she knew what I had going on in Chicago, but I didn't care enough to figure it out. I was just willing to do what I needed to get Jarrah to forgive me and take me back. I knew helping Isabelle kidnap her was low even for me, but I didn't expect her life to be consistently in danger. Isabelle assured me Jarrah would remain untouched until we got the money we were going after. However, Jarrah had been suffering constantly, and the worst thing that came out of all of this was Mama's death from bone cancer. Although Mama Charmaine put Dario up to killing me, she was still my mama, and I still loved her. It hurt me that she didn't trust me enough to tell me she was dying. I was in Atlanta with her all of this time, and I didn't know. I should have known. If that weren't bad enough, I couldn't even attend her funeral to grieve her death because I was supposed to be dead. It was hard as hell to stay away from Jarrah during that time because I knew she needed me as much as I needed her. Losing Mama was something I never saw coming. She was there for me most of my life, so I got used to her being around. Not being able to call her every day was tough. Even with the bad blood between us, I still loved her as my mother. I stood over the twins' mother and stared at her as she lay unconscious on my sofa.

"So, what's next," Donald asked me, breaking my concentration.

"I call Jarrah and demand a trade. She won't be able to deny me when she finds out I got her play mother," I explained. He nodded and sat down on the other end of the sofa. I hoped Jarrah would choose me because life as I knew it before she left me was over. I was going to lose my hotels, my apartment, my new Lincoln MKX, and possibly my position in my company if I couldn't prove I didn't sexually harass that bitch Kiandra. Getting Jarrah back was the only thing I had control of, so I hope things went my way. I knew the twins would come after her since she left Chicago, and if I were right, they should have been at Mama Charmaine's house already. I dug into the front right pocket on my Banana Republic jeans and retrieved my cell phone. Then, I dialed Jarrah's number. My hands trembled a bit as I held the phone to my ear and waited for her to answer.

"Hello," Jarrah hesitantly said through the phone. I could tell she was shocked to hear from me. She didn't even know I was still alive. The twins didn't get a chance to tell her with everything going on. My heart palpitated at the sound of her soft, slightly high-pitched voice. I hadn't realized how long it had been since I last spoke to her. That was the day I found out she was pregnant. Leaving the hospital with that news crushed me. That was what pushed me to work with Isabelle. I felt betrayed. I knew she didn't do it on purpose, but I couldn't help but be disappointed in her. She and I were supposed to have a family together. She wasn't supposed to have another man's baby. I discreetly breathed in and out as I tried to focus on the task at hand. I needed to handle my business, so Donald could stop following me around like he was my shadow. I knew he wanted revenge for Summer, but he was starting to get on my nerves. However, I had to keep my promise to him since he saved my life.

"Hello there, wifey! It's been a long time since I heard your voice," I said into the phone. I knew hearing my voice would give her a sense of relief because no matter what, Jarrah would never wish death on me.

"How are you… how are you still alive," she questioned, confirming my assumptions. Hearing how she reacted to my being alive made me feel like I had a fair chance.

"It was a miracle. My guardian angel kept me from taking a trip to the spirit realm. I'm surprised Thing One and Thing Two didn't fill you in," I remarked, throwing them under the bus for not telling her I was alive. She paused for several seconds.

"Your angel," she finally inquired, rhetorically. I knew she knew I was referring to her, but she wanted clarity, and I wanted nothing more than to give it to her.

"Yes, Jarrah. When I was fighting for my life, you were my motivation to stay alive. So, in a way, you saved me. That means you are my purpose. Whether you believe it or not, we are supposed to be together," I declared. I could hear her suck her teeth through the phone and got nervous for a brief second.

"Quincy, you were the one that divorced me, not the other way around. So, you don't get to say that to me," she stated. I silently thought about what she said. She was right, but I did that with the belief that I could always get her back. If someone had told me a year ago that she would be with someone else, I would not have believed it. It was shocking to me, and my ego wouldn't allow me to accept it.

"Enough of that. We'll have plenty of time to discuss our relationship. Right now, I have something more important to discuss with you… and the twins. I'm sure they're there by now. You should put me on speaker, so we can discuss things together," I told her, changing the subject. I didn't want to have that discussion with her in front of everyone.

I could hear Jarrah taking the phone from her ear and pressing the speaker phone button. I swallowed the lump in my throat and stood up so I could speak with conviction. I needed to send a message to them, so they would take me seriously.

"You're on, Q," Jarrah announced to me.

"What's up, fellas? It's about time we put an end to this war we got going on."

"What do you want," Dario asked me. I had gotten good at telling them apart by the way they spoke. Dario was more ghetto than Dustin, so he was louder and more aggressive in his tone.

"What do I want? Are you serious? You know damn well what I want, and if you knew what I know, you'd damn well give it to me," I threatened as I eyed their mother.

"I will die before I ever hand Jarrah over to your sick ass. You're out of your fucking mind. Those bullets I put into your head must have given you brain damage," Dario spat. I let out an ominous laugh because he was a joke to me, always acting tough.

"Actually, those bullets were more persistent than you were with murdering me. I did sustain some damage to my brain, but nothing is going to stop me from getting my wife back," I declared.

"Jarrah isn't your wife. You fucked that up, and I will never allow you to take her away from me again,"

Dario barked. I had successfully gotten under his skin, and it was amusing to me.

"Say what you want, but that woman… and that child belong to me. If you want to see your immigrant mother again… then you'd give her back to me," I demanded while revealing I had their mother. They were silent for several seconds.

"If something happens to my mama, I will put you in the dirt again, nigga," Dustin snarled like a beast, shocking me. Dustin wasn't usually the rowdy one out of the pair.

"I'll be damned if I let you take my girl, and my child away from me," Dustin added. I could tell he was fed up with my shit, but I didn't care. I wanted what I wanted, and no one was going to scare me out of it.

"Enough," Jarrah yelled at us. We all grew silent. I hadn't even realized we were bickering with each other like some bitches while she just sat there and listened. I started to feel bad as I realized we were treating her like she was a trophy we believed should sit our mantles.

"I'm not some fucking toy you get to pass around. This decision is mine, and all of you will do what the fuck I say," Jarrah chastised. We didn't have a choice but to eat our words after that. She was prepared to lay down the law for us. I could hear it in her voice.

"Bout time, shorty. Tell them niggas how shit gone go," Jerrell interjected. I rolled my eyes. I disliked him because Isabelle told me everything, she had him do for her. He was dangerous, yet somehow, he was able to win Jarrah over. I was sure the twins didn't like it as much as I didn't.

"Quincy, we won't be making a trade. You will bring Annalise back to me, and you will leave here without me," Jarrah commanded. My jaw dropped as I witnessed her standing up for herself. I wasn't used to seeing this side of her.

"I am interested in repairing our relationship, but only as friends. You made the decision to divorce me, so you have to suffer the consequences of that. I understand you're lonely, and you want me around to fill the void you have inside you, but I'm not going to continue to be your crutch. I love you, and I 'm happy you're alive, but I will never be your wife again. All I have to offer you is friendship, so either you take it or leave it. You will bring Ms. Anna back, though, or I'll hunt you down myself and put you out of your misery for good. Understand," she asked me. I was at a loss for words. This woman I was speaking to was different from the one I was married to. The statement she made was bittersweet. I was happy to hear she still loved me and was happy I was alive but hearing her say she'd never be my wife again hurt me, but I'd rather have piece of her than not have her at all.

"Fine. I want to see you when I bring her back, though. I promise I'm not going to try anything. I just… I need to see you," I admitted to her, as I fought back tears. I had been acting like a maniac when at the end of the day, I just missed my best friend. Jarrah and I had been inseparable since the day we met, so it was hard being without her. We did everything together, so I would be doing something as simple as washing the dishes, and I would remember things about our life together. She was a huge part of my life, and I wasn't ready to let her go, but I didn't have a choice. She made her decision, so all I could do was accept it. I had grown tired of going to war with them anyway. It was turning me into someone I wasn't, and it was draining. I was ready to wave the white flag.

"Okay. I'm okay with that," she finally responded. I let out a loud sigh of relief. More than anything, I wanted to see Jarrah so I could hold her in my arms. I missed her. It had been over a year since I'd held her in my arms, and so much happened. We lost our earthly angel, and I wanted to grieve our mother's death with her.

"Thank you, Jarrah. I'm bringing your mother back right now. I'll be there in a few minutes," I immediately replied. I didn't care about anything else. I knew Donald and Deandra would be mad at me, but I didn't care. Jarrah was willing to repair our relationship, so that's all I needed to know.

"Okay, I'll see you when you get here. I need to talk to the twins, so I'm hanging up with you," Jarrah told me. Then, we said our goodbyes. I looked over at Donald. I could tell he wasn't pleased with what he overheard, but I couldn't care less. At the end of the day, he didn't even like his sister like that, so getting revenge shouldn't have mattered to him that much. If it still did, he could continue to go after Dario. He just had to do it without me because I was done with this revenge shit. Jarrah was all I wanted in the first place. She extended a friendship to me, so that meant our story wasn't over yet.

Chapter 2: BFF

February 10, 2017
Sugarcane Valley
Atlanta, Georgia

After hanging up with Jarrah, I went to the medical bag Deandra gave me, and retrieved the naloxone nasal spray from it so I could administer it to Annalise. Donald and I didn't give her a heavy dose of morphine. We only gave her enough to put her to sleep. I inserted the nasal spray inside her right nostril, so I could wake her up. I didn't want Jarrah to know I drugged her, so I hoped this spray worked. If not, it would be something else for her to be angry with me about, and I didn't want to alter what she agreed to before we even got to see each other. After about a minute, Annalise gasped, and sat up like she was possessed. She must have been dizzy because she ended up laying back on the couch. I didn't know anything about the medicine Deandra gave me, but I followed the instructions she gave me perfectly. She did tell me there were symptoms, so maybe that's what was going on with Annalise. I stood over her and looked in her face to make sure she was okay. Her eyelashes fluttered like butterfly wings as she blinked to clear her vision.

"Are you okay," I asked her. She stared at me for a few seconds. Then, suddenly, she slapped the fuck out of me. I was so caught off guard by it my eyes bucked, and my mouth parted like I was about to scream. I held my cheek and turned my attention to Donald to see if he had witnessed what happened, and he was laughing at me.

"That's what you get for being soft, *hijoputa,*" Donald teased. I shook my head and slowly turned my attention back to Annalise. She had successfully sat up this time.

"What did you two do to me," she asked us as she frowned at us.

"We just injected you with enough morphine to put you to sleep. You should be fine after getting some rest and drinking some water," I told her as I handed her a bottle of Fiji water from the twelve pack I had in my refrigerator. She eyed the water for a few seconds before she broke the seal and drank some of it. Then, she sneezed a few times. I figured that was a side effect of the nasal spray. I went into my guest bathroom and got her some tissue because her nose was running.

"You good," I asked her while standing a few inches from her this time. I didn't want a taste of what she gave me the first time. She bowed her head twice to answer me.

"Good. I'm going to take you back to Jarrah now. We've worked things out already," I explained to her. She nodded at me again.

"Speak for yourself," Donald mumbled under his breath. I rolled my eyes at him but ignored him. He was acting like he cared so much when I know he didn't. He could have easily taken the lead role in this plot, yet he didn't. He told me his family was in The Mexican Mafia, but I thought it was fishy he didn't go straight for Dario's head in that case. He knew Dario killed Summer because he was the one who found me. I really didn't care about his family business, though. After resolving things with Jarrah, I was going to part ways with him.

"Are you okay to walk," I asked Annalise. She stood up slowly, and stepped forward to see if she could walk alone, but she stumbled. I caught her before she could fall.

"It's okay. I got you," I told her as I held her up. Then, we walked to the front door.

"Follow us in my Mama's car," I commanded Donald before I carried Annalise outside to my car. After about two minutes, he emerged from my apartment, and got in Mama Charmaine's car. I cranked my car up and drove to her house where Jarrah and the twins were.

"Why are you taking me back? What happened," Annalise questioned as she looked at me through the rearview mirror. She refused to sit in front with me. I didn't care, though. Her forgiveness was not what I was seeking, so she didn't offend me by keeping her distance.

"Jarrah made me a proposal I couldn't deny. If I'm being honest, she didn't give me a choice. She demanded I bring you back, and told me she wasn't leaving with me, but she did agree to repair our relationship, so I accepted her proposal," I elaborated. Annalise smiled to herself. I could tell from her glowing smile she was proud of Jarrah for ending the war. She didn't say anything else to me after that. We continued to ride to Sugarcane Valley in silence.

After ten minutes, we pulled up to Jarrah and my childhood home. Jarrah must have heard us coming because she came outside and stood on the deck. I was happy she came out alone. I guess she understood I desperately wanted to see her. It had been a year and a half since I saw her without someone else standing in the way. I made my bed when I divorced her, so I knew I had to lie in it by myself, but since she was willing to give me access to her meant a lot to me. It would take me some time to accept that we would never be like we were again, but eventually I would. I just wanted to hold the only woman I ever loved in my arms to show her I still loved her. Ms. Annalise got out of the car before I could put it in park. I knew she was relieved to see Jarrah again. Technically, we kidnapped her, so I was sure she was a bit traumatized. I couldn't say I cared about her at all. I was only calling a truce for Jarrah, and no one else. I slowly got out of the car and walked toward Jarrah. After climbing the steps, I stood aside on the deck as she had her moment with Annalise who was struggling to stand up straight like a drunkard. I could tell Jarrah noticed it, but Annalise was trying to hide it from her. She must not have wanted Jarrah to worry about her. I was thankful to her because I didn't want Jarrah to know we drugged her. I would rather spare myself of a lecture and spend this moment connecting with my wife.

"*Mi hija,* I knew you would fix everything. I'm so proud of you," she exclaimed, before kissing her on the cheek. I rolled my eyes internally. I'll admit that I was jealous of watching her receive the love I craved from Jarrah. Witnessing the new family, she created with them made me feel like she abandoned me, but I knew the state of our relationship was all my fault. I just wished I did things differently. However, I couldn't turn back the hands of time.

"Are you okay," Jarrah asked Annalise as she held her hands and stared into her eyes. I cringed as I envied the bond they built. It seemed like Annalise was trying to replace our mother, and I didn't like it.

"I'm a little dizzy, but I'm fine," she convinced Jarrah. Jarrah opened the door for her, so she could go inside. I knew the twins would be able to tell their mother was drugged, but as long as they didn't come out here trying to press me about it, we were cool. Besides, I didn't harm her. I simply allowed Donald to inject her with morphine. As long as she took it easy, she would be fine. At least that's what Deandra explained to me when I questioned her about it. I wanted to be completely sure I didn't kill anyone by accident. I kept my hands clean the entire time in case something popped off. I may have been a menace to the twins, Jarrah, and Theresa, but prison wasn't for me. I would fold immediately in there and probably off myself.

When Jarrah and I were alone, we stared at each other in silence for a few minutes. "You're still as beautiful as I remember," I complimented, making her smile broadly and angelically. My heart fluttered at the sight of her straight radiant white teeth. I was glad she was being warm and inviting to me although I didn't deserve it.

"You know, all you had to tell me was that you missed me. I would have met with you," Jarrah informed me. I flashed her a closed mouthed one cheek smile. I knew I could have just followed-up with her after she got out of the hospital, but by the time that happened, Isabelle had already contacted me. I never figured out how she knew me or how she found me, but she was the one that got into my head. I was already feeling some type of way about Jarrah and Dario's pregnancy news, so it was easy for her to manipulate me into doing her dirty work. I was stupid and vulnerable. Plus, I needed the money to pay back The Reapers, so I joined her. She easily resolved my debt with Matteo Palermo, making me her new slave. I was glad she got killed because I would have still been on her leash.

"Those were my plans, but my ego got the best of me," I acknowledged. I knew I had to be honest with Jarrah if I wanted to continue to have a relationship with her. She was the only family I had left. Our beloved Mama Charmaine died, my birth mother was dead to me, and I allowed Deandra to kidnap Marcus, so I was alone.

"Next time, just ask. I almost lost you because of your ego," Jarrah said as tears escaped her big doe eyes. I immediately pulled her into my arms and held onto her so tight you couldn't tell where I ended, and she began. I hated that I caused her pain. I was just so lost without her I was acting out of character. I lost so much in the past two years, I hated to lose the best thing that's ever happened to me. I locked my arms around Jarrah's waist and prepared to convey my feelings to her.

"I'm so sorry, Jarrah. I'm sorry I put you through all of this, and I'm so sorry I wasn't there with you when

Mama died. I didn't know she was sick. I promise you if I did, I'd do everything in my power to save her, but she hid it from me too. I knew you left her here because you thought I would take care of her, but I failed you. I swear I'm going to be a better man. Please forgive me," I pleaded. She snuggled into my arms like a puppy, and we cried together. I could feel Mama's pride encircling the two of us. I knew she'd be happy we got things figured out and surrendered to each other's love. Mama Charmaine was the glue that held us together, even when we were apart. So, losing her was hard for all of us, even Theresa. I may not have been on good terms with her, but I could admit that the three of us needed to hold onto what Mama instilled in us, and squash all the beef between us. I never thought I would say it, but I hoped, with time, Terry and I could reconcile our differences. Mama would have wanted us to keep our family together in her absence.

Jarrah and I dried each other's tears after we released each other. It felt good to pour my heart out to her as we grieved Mama Charmaine's death. She created a small family for us since we were broken kids in need of love, and I wanted us to always be family regardless of anything else.

"Quincy, I'm not able to forgive you right away, but… I meant what I said. I do want to repair our relationship. I'll be here for a little while, so maybe we can have that lunch you offered me," Jarrah proposed after our tears stopped. I smiled and bowed my head. She didn't forgive me immediately, but that didn't mean she never would. I just had to give her time. The things she went through because of me were uncalled for, and not deserved. So, I needed to suffer the consequences of that.

"I'd like that! Take care of yourself, Jarrah," I told her. Then, I hugged her again, and kissed her forehead after letting her go. Having this time with her put a lot of things into perspective for me. There were a lot of things I needed to change about myself. I had been so selfish I pushed away the only person who loved me without expecting anything in return. It was going to be hard adjusting to not having her as my wife, but I was open to learning how to be her friend again. It would be a challenge, but I was up for it. Besides, I needed to let her go, and stop using her as a crutch like she said. I desperately needed to spend some time alone so I could figure myself out.

"You do the same, Q," Jarrah called out to me as she stood on the deck and watched me leave. After I got in my car, Donald pulled up in Mama Charmaine's car. I hadn't realized he wasn't there the whole time I was speaking with Jarrah. There was something suspicious about his actions. However, I decided to keep my mouth closed for now. Once he gave Jarrah the keys to our mother's car, he got in the passenger side of my 2015 Lincoln MKX and put on his seatbelt. I took one last look at Jarrah before I drove off. I didn't know how things were going to end when I decided to go to Chicago to win Jarrah back. I definitely didn't think she would move on so soon, and with two successful black men who I aspired to be like. I shook my head as I thought of all I went through to get her back, only to end up with nothing. Donald and I rode back to my apartment in silence. I wanted to ask him why it took him so long to get to Mama Charmaine's house, but I didn't. I knew I had to stay on my toes when I was dealing with him. He was built differently, and his family was dangerous. I had gotten myself into some deep shit when I aligned myself with Deandra and him, but I was no longer going to let them pull me under. I had a second chance at life, so I was going to live it the way I wanted to.

Chapter 3: A New Lease on Life

February 15, 2017
The Carter Hotel
Atlanta, Georgia

I never thought I'd be happy about spending the majority of my money, I chuckled as I looked over my finances with my accountant and felt relieved. After seeing Jarrah, I decided to get my life together. Once I called Deandra to tell her about the truce so she would let Marcus go, I paid off all of my debt as soon as the weekend was over. I took care of the business loans with the bank for my hotels, my apartment rent for a full year, all of the gambling debt I accumulated over time, and I paid off my new 2015 Lincoln MKX so I wouldn't have to worry about it getting repossessed if I fell on demanding times. I knew I needed to build a new relationship with money since I was bad with it, so I decided I wouldn't make any big purchases or apply for any more loans without consulting my accountant first. Before, Jarrah was the one who dealt with our finances, so I didn't even bother to get to know our accountant, Aurora. However, I was a single man, so I had to handle my own business. It would be hard, but I had some things in order for me to stay on track. I was down to five hundred and seventy-five thousand dollars, but I knew I had it in me to make that six million back. I had to put my pride and fear to the side to get back everything I lost. I had the funds to take care of it in the first place. I just didn't want to lose the wealth and status I earned through hard work and support from Jarrah. It was bittersweet, but it had to be done if I wanted to return to the peaceful life I had before I created marital problems for Jarrah and me.

I hadn't seen Jarrah in a few days, but we kept in contact through text message. She was still in Atlanta taking care of Mama Charmaine's business, so I had time to spend with her before she went back to Chicago. Jarrah told me she was planning to have a ceremony to spread Mama's ashes, so her family could send her off in the right way. Since the funeral was held in Chicago, many of Mama Charmaine's family didn't get to mourn her death. I was glad she invited me to the ceremony because I needed to say goodbye to my mother, so I could move on. I had forgiven her for what she did to me in the moment, so there wasn't any unfinished business between us. I immediately understood why she betrayed me. I caused Jarrah a lot of trouble and pain, and Mama Charmaine knew her time would be up soon, so she got rid of me in hopes that Jarrah would be safe from harm after she left. It was her way of making sure she would be able to rest in peace. That was something I couldn't hold a grudge over. Mama Charmaine loved me more than my own mother did, so hating her wasn't even an option for me. However, it was necessary for me to mourn her death with Jarrah because I had a lot of healing I needed to do and grieving her would jumpstart my journey.

"Okay, Mr. Carter. It looks like we have everything back in order," Aurora announced to me through a warm smile. It felt good to be financially stable after having to give up most of my money. The money was a reminder of how far I had come, so I didn't want to think about losing it all. To me, it meant that I was losing my power. As black men, we didn't often get opportunities to gain wealth in the system that was against us. Yet, we were expected to be providers. So, I struggled to give up the wealth I'd worked so hard for. In my mind, money equaled power, so if I didn't have any money, my power would be gone. That was a hard pill to swallow, especially since I had it. I knew it was my fault I lost everything, but it still pained me to go through it.

"You don't know how happy I am to hear that," I smiled, urging her to mirror me.

"I do this for a living, so I have a clever idea how you felt going through what you went through. At least you had the money to pay your debt off, though. Most people don't. They end up losing it all, and most never get it back. But don't worry, Mr. Carter... I'll keep your finances in order, so you won't have to go through that again," she assured me. I sighed deeply.

"Good. I'm glad I can count on you," I replied. It felt good to be debt free. I just had to build my riches up again. As I looked toward my future, Mama Charmaine's voice echoed in my head. "If you got it once, you could get it again." She would always tell Jarrah and I that when our money would get low from me gambling it away, and she was right because we always got it back. Although I didn't have Jarrah's help anymore, I had to believe I could do it without her.

"Absolutely! Well, Mr. Carter... our business here is done. I'll be leaving since I have an appointment with another client," Aurora told me as she gathered her things. I stood up to escort her out the door like the gentleman I was.

Before we left out of my office, she looked back at me, and said, "Now that you're an eligible bachelor, what are you going to do about a companion?"

I was caught off guard by her question since she was wearing a wedding ring. "Uh... I don't know. I haven't thought about it yet. I'm still trying to get my life together," I responded.

"I see. You should figure that out. I'm sure there are plenty of women who would like their chance with you. Excuse my bluntness, but if I weren't married, I would be in line," she admitted. I smirked at her. I couldn't believe she was flirting with me.

I stepped in closer to her as I continued to hold the door, and said, "I'll keep that in mind." Then, I seductively licked my thin lips as she stared into my eyes.

Aurora Torres was fine as hell. She was Filipino and Black, and she reminded me of the rapper, Mila J, but her skin was a deep lustrous yellow that looked golden. Her striking chestnut brown eyes reeled me in, the moment I saw her, and her small prominent nose, dainty soft pink lips, and chiseled bone structure made me weak in the knees like an R&B singer. This was my first-time meeting Aurora since Jarrah was the one who dealt with her, so I was unaware that she was this sexy. She tucked a small piece of her jet-black wavy hair behind her ear as she looked up at me and bit into her delicious looking bottom lip. She had an innocent face, but I had a feeling she was anything but that. It took so much out of me to refrain from kissing her. I knew she hesitated so I could make a move, but I backed down like a pussy. It was crazy to me that I had no issue cheating on Jarrah while we were together, but all of a sudden, I'd become considerate of her feelings. I knew she told me we would never get back together, but I had to try again before I started putting myself out there to date other women. Plus, I learned my lesson not to mix business with pleasure after Kiandra lied on me. Luckily, I had gotten that situation sorted out.

Fortunately for me, the cameras inside my hotel were enough to show Human Resources I didn't harass her. We did have sex, but she initiated it with me every time we had it, so she didn't get away with trying to ruin my reputation because I didn't want to wife her. Her dumb ass thought she was going to take Jarrah's place, but no woman could ever hold a candle to Jarrah in my mind. Not even the fine ass Blasian goddess who was in close proximity of me. Aurora was enticing as hell, but I didn't feel like I was ready to move on just yet, especially since she was my accountant. I didn't care that she was married because I didn't take my own vows seriously. However, I wanted to stop being impulsive like I had been in the past. I made so many mistakes in the name of doing what I wanted to do and being *the man*. Losing Jarrah taught me I had a habit of sabotaging myself when I doubted that I deserved all I had. Even though I wasn't with her, I felt like I owed it to Jarrah to change into the man she believed I could be, and I didn't think I could do that while I was fucking every woman that showed some interest in me. Once Aurora realized I wasn't picking up what she was putting down, she smirked and walked out of my office. I escorted her all the way to her car.

"Nice meeting you, Mr. Carter. I look forward to seeing more of you," she told me. We locked eyes for a few seconds. Then, she put on her seatbelt, shut her car door, and drove off as I stood kicking myself for not taking the chance, she gave me to kiss her pretty ass lips. I shook my head at my damn self. Being a changed man was already a challenge. I put my hands in my pants pockets and walked back into my hotel. It was colder than usual for Georgia this time of year. I hated wintry weather.

Having to deal with snow and dry air in Chicago was enough for me for six winters. I was happy to be home in Atlanta. This was where I belonged, regardless of if Jarrah was with me or not. However, since The Carter I, II, and III were back in my possession, and I didn't owe any money on them, I was thinking about allowing Dario and Dustin to finish my hotel in Chicago. It was always a dream of mine to own a hotel in the city where my father was born. I didn't have many memories of him, but I wanted to do something that would make me feel close to him. Both of my parents failed me as a kid, but Jarrah and Mama instilled good traits in me. I wanted to be the man they saw me as. Not just for them, but for myself too. I was doing myself a disservice by wasting my second chance getting revenge on the twins for taking Jarrah from me. I realized they didn't take her from me. I gave her to them when I called myself punishing her with the divorce. I was stupid to think a woman as beautiful, intelligent, kind, and loyal as Jarrah wouldn't be sought after by many men. Jarrah was always going to be my biggest fuckup. She loved me unconditionally, but I didn't give her that in return. Truthfully, I didn't know how. I was a broken man. No matter how much love, patience, and compassion they showed me, I was still as fucked up as I was when I was a little boy.

When I got to my desk, I picked up my phone to check my notifications. My eyes widened when I saw two missed calls from Jarrah. I should have taken my phone with me, but instead of beating myself up about it, I just called her back. The phone rang a few times before she answered. "Hello," she said through the phone with her soft, high-pitched voice. Her voice still gave me chills.

"Hello. I'm sorry for missing your calls. I was meeting with my accountant," I immediately explained to her.

"That's okay, Q. I know you're a busy man," she giggled. I chuckled.

"Well, I have been busy cleaning up this mess I made," I confessed, but she didn't respond.

"What's up, though? Why did you call," I inquired.

"I wanted to see if you were free to have lunch with me tomorrow. I'm going back to Chicago in a few days, so I figured we could get together before I leave," she explained. I smiled so hard my cheek muscles burned.

"Of course! You know I'll make time for my w-" I was about to say, but I paused mid-sentence to correct myself.

"I meant you. I'll make time for you," I said. Jarrah giggled.

"Mmhmm. I bet. Anyways, you know where I want to meet, so I don't have to tell you. I'm free all day, so we can make it an all-day thing. I want us to release Mama's ashes together," she told me. I raised my right eyebrow. I was excited she wanted to spend the full day with me, but I thought she was having a ceremony for Mama Charmaine's whole family to attend.

"Wait! I thought you were planning a bigger ceremony. What happened," I questioned. Jarrah was silent for several seconds. Then, she inhaled deeply, paused for a second, then exhaled deeply. I could tell something was up.

"What's going on, Jarrah?"

"Not much. I just... I'm not in the mental space to entertain a bunch of people. I know they're my family, but I'm exhausted physically and mentally. I've been through so much lately. I just want to do something simple. Since we were the closest to her, I figured we could do an intimate ceremony with just us. I invited Terry, but she couldn't make it. She's not feeling well, so it's just you and me," Jarrah elaborated. Hearing her say she was drained mentally and physically made me feel bad because I caused her a lot of pain recently. She'd been nothing but nice to me, and I fucked up her peace. I didn't know how yet, but I was going to do something to show her my deepest apologies for interfering with her life while she was happy with someone else.

"Okay, then. I guess I'll see you tomorrow. I'll take the day off, so I can spend time with you," I replied, deciding not to make a big deal of what she shared with me. Instead, I'd just show her an enjoyable time to get her mind off it.

"You sure. I don't want you to miss out on anything important because of me," she asked me. I shook my head like she could see me through the phone.

"I'm sure, Jarrah. I owe you so much more," I acknowledged. Silence befell us for a few lengthy seconds.

"You don't owe me anything, Quincy. I know what you did was wrong, but… all you need to do to pay me back is change. That's all I want from you." I fidgeted with my hair as I thought about what she said. Regardless, I was going to make up for what I did. I didn't know how yet, but I would figure it out, though.

"That's not true. I owe you everything, and there's nothing you can do or say for me to think otherwise. What I did to you was unforgivable. I know that, so I want to redeem myself," I confessed.

"Q? Can this conversation wait until I see you?" I thought it was weird of her to ask me that, but I assumed one of the twins walked into the room with her, and she didn't want to talk to me in front of them. Either way, I would get to tell her everything I wanted to say in person, so that was best for me.

"Okay, I understand. I'll see you tomorrow."

"Okay, Q. Enjoy the rest of your day," she told me, before we got off the phone. I hated hearing that Jarrah was going through it. I wasn't solely responsible for everything that happened to her, but I was still holding myself accountable for the part I played in making her life as hard as it had been. Even though we ended things, Jarrah was going to be dealing with what we did to her for a while. The fact that she was okay with being friends with me was insane. I didn't deserve anything from her, but she deserved everything from me, and I was going to figure out how to give it to her.

Chapter 4: Old Love

February 16, 2017
Atlanta Breakfast Club
Atlanta, Georgia

As I parked my Lincoln MKX in the parking lot of Atlanta Breakfast Club, my palms were so sweaty they were slipping off the steering wheel. I reached over to my glove compartment and got some napkins out of it to wipe my hands and the steering wheel off. I didn't understand why I was nervous like this was my first date with Jarrah. I just saw her a few days ago, so it wasn't like it had been a while since we last seen each other. I guess I was just anxious about how things would go. Jarrah and I didn't have the best experiences with each other the past few years of our relationship. I treated her so bad she got so fed up with me that she got violent with me during one of our many arguments. It was shocking to both of us because we went our whole lives together without putting our hands on each other. She beat herself up about it for a long time, and even though she was the one who put her hands on me, I didn't give her flack for it. I knew I provoked her to that point. I was out in the streets living recklessly. I had been sleeping around so much I gave her chlamydia twice in a row. That was a tough time for us, so it was surreal things were coming full circle.

Jarrah and I had a lot of difficulties in our relationship from the beginning, so being able to be cordial with her after everything that went down was amazing to me. I needed to get over my nerves because Jarrah had been nothing but nice to me. I switched my car off, unbuckled my seatbelt, and got out. I stood in front of my car and scanned the parking lot for Mama Charmaine's car, but I didn't see it. As I was pulling my phone out of my pocket, she snuck up on me, and stood in front of me. When I realized she was near, our eyes met, and I was instantly mesmerized by her hazel eyes, and that beautiful iridescent smile she exhibited to me. Jarrah looked amazing in the mocha-colored cable knit button down cardigan cropped sweater with bat sleeves, chocolate high waisted skinny jeans, and dark brown platform Steve Madden booties she was wearing. She also donned a yellow gold diamond ear sleeve, chocker, and matching bracelet, and Playboy bunny nose cuff that accentuated her caramel complexion. She was dressed casually, but she still blew me away. I could tell she gained weight, but it looked so good on her. Even better than her normal size. I was speechless as we gazed into each other's eyes. It felt like I was meeting her for the first time. Her energy was different, but still as pure as it always was.

"Hey," she said to me, casting a spell on me. I forgot the power she had over me with just her presence alone.

"Hey yourself! You look beautiful as hell," I intentionally told her as I looked her up and down. She giggled as she pushed her hair behind her ear like she was nervous.

"Thank you! You look amazing yourself," she responded. I was wearing a heather gray turtleneck sweater under a maroon blazer that I wore open, navy-blue slacks, and all black velvet slip on Giorgio Armani shoes. It was about sixty-five degrees, so it wasn't cold enough for me to wear a jacket. I got up at eight this morning to go to my barber to get my signature low fade, but this time, I got my hair cut down low instead of wearing my mini afro. I wanted to look my best since I was going to be in the presence of the most beautiful woman I had ever seen. Jarrah's beauty was effortless, so I needed to look extra good to stand next to her, and not be completely invisible.

"Thanks! I had to wear my Sunday's best 'cause I knew you'd look gorgeous regardless of what you were wearing," I replied. She grinned bashfully but remained quiet.

"Let's get in here before we miss our table," I told her as I held my arm out for her. She interlocked her arm into mine before we walked into the restaurant. When we were in front of the host, I gave her my information for the reservations I made after getting off the phone with Jarrah yesterday, and she immediately got a waitress to escort us to our table. Once we were there, I pulled Jarrah's chair out and helped her in her seat before sitting in mine.

"Thank you, Mr. Carter," she told me when we both were seated. I smiled and I nodded at her.

"Are you two ready to put in your drink orders or do you need time," the waitress asked while handing us our menus.

"Actually, a menu isn't even necessary," I responded as I looked up at the waitress and prepared to give her our orders. Jarrah and I ate there enough for me to know her order by heart. She loved the food here, but she always ordered the same thing every time we went.

"Okay sir. I'm ready when you are," the waitress told me.

"My… date will have the Southern Breakfast with scrambled eggs, bacon, breakfast potatoes, and the biscuit with a side of peach cobbler French toast. I will have Breakfast Tacos with two extra tacos and the Gulf Shrimp and Grits with extra butter and cheese. For our drinks, she'll have apple juice and water, and I'll coffee with three sugars and two creamers," I recited overused lines. I could see Jarrah staring at me out the corner of my eyes.

"Will that be all," the waitress asked us. I looked at Jarrah to make sure I got her order right. She smiled at me and nodded to assure me I was on point. I smiled internally at myself for remembering her order. I felt like it gave me some cool points with her at least.

"Yes, that will be all. Thank you," I finally responded.

"Okay! I will be right out with your orders as soon as they're done," the waitress assured us before she left the table. Jarrah and I stared at each other in silence for at least a minute. It was dreamlike to be sitting in front of her after everything that went down between us. I felt horrible for what I took her through, but I was so thankful she didn't turn her back on me. I didn't know what I would have done if I had to live without her in my life. Even though she was technically in a relationship with the twins, I still loved her the same.

"So, how have things been going with you, Q," she queried, breaking the light silence between us.

"Things are decent. I'm in the process of getting my life together since I completely ruined it after you left," I replied.

"Well, I saw that coming a mile away," she teased. I chuckled.

"Yet, you still left me," I retorted. She shrugged her shoulders and smirked.

"You gave me the out, so I ran as fast as I could."

"Wow! That's how you gone do me," I asked. Although she was joking, what she said stung me a little bit.

"I mean, you did it to yourself, Mr. My Way Or The Highway," she said as she rolled her neck. I laughed at her.

"I wasn't that bad."

"Shiiiddd," she responded. We laughed hysterically. I forgot how effortlessly funny Jarrah was. It was one of the things I loved about her. I stared deeply into her eyes as our laughter died down. Moments like these were what I missed the most about her.

"Fair enough. I guess I deserved that... and everything else that happened to me after what I did to you. I should be on my hands and knees thanking you for sparing me. I know the twins would put an end to me in an instance if you wanted me gone. I got the scar to prove what they're capable of," I said, immediately changing the mood. Jarrah traced my scar with her eyes, and I could see the pity glistening in her hazel eyes.

"How are you? I mean, how is it living with that," she inquired. I inhaled deeply and exhaled loudly after holding my breath for ten seconds. I wanted to avoid this conversation today and focus my attention on sharing this last moment with her before she left, but I knew it would come up.

"Well… let's just say I'll be dealing with the trauma from almost losing my life for a while. I really thought I was invincible, but that bullet humbled me really quickly. I was acting tough, but I was scared as hell of it happening again. Although I backed down for you, I have to admit that the thought of me dying had something to do with why I surrendered so easily when you asked me to. I was never a tough guy to begin with, so I don't know what got into me to make me act that way. I was just so afraid of losing you forever. I knew it was my fault you were gone, but I honestly didn't think you would move on so soon. I thought I had time to fuck around for a while, but when I realized shit wasn't what I thought it would be, I panicked. I was willing to do anything to get you back," I confessed. Jarrah bit her pouty bottom lip as she stared at me. I reached across the table and swiped a few tears from underneath her eye before they could caress her cheek. She pressed the back of her hand into her eye to stop the tears from falling.

"I'm sorry for making you cry, Jarrah. It wasn't my intention. I just-"

"It's okay, Quincy. I'm not mad at you for being honest. How could I be? I just wish things didn't happen this way. You were my best friend. Losing you drove me crazy," Jarrah admitted. Although I already knew that it felt good to hear her say it. However, I wasn't okay with making her cry. I pulled a few napkins out of the dispenser and reached across the table to pat her eyes dry. She allowed me to do it for a few seconds before she grabbed the napkin herself.

"You deserved so much more from me after everything you've done for me, but I was too selfish and arrogant to give it to you. After all the love Mama and you gave me, I'm still incapable of reciprocating it. Sometimes, I feel like I'm broken beyond repair. Monalisa's mistakes really fucked me up. I hate her for the way she brought me into this world just to instill all of these bad qualities in me," I sighed. Jarrah shook her head.

"Don't say that Q. You don't mean it. You don't hate your mother."

"But I do. I do hate her, Jarrah," I reiterated. Jarrah frowned. I knew it broke her heart to hear me say it, but it was the truth. My mother wasn't anything like Mama Charmaine. She hated me from the time she gave birth to me. I could feel it even as a kid.

"I'm sorry she wasn't what you needed her to be, but it's not too late for you, Q. You can be a better man," she encouraged me. I lowered my gaze. I didn't know if there was much truth in that, but I was damn sure going to give it my all for both of us.

"I know. That's why I made an appointment to see a therapist," I confessed. Jarrah's eyes bucked as she met my gaze. I could tell she was both shocked and proud of me for taking that step all on my own.

"Wow! You really are cleaning your life up. I'm so proud of you Q," she exclaimed all at once. I couldn't help but chuckle at her.

"I don't know whether I should be happy you're proud or feel some type of way that you're shocked." We both laughed.

"I mean surprise aside… I really am proud of you, Quincy. I always knew you could do it yourself. Monalisa may have been many things, but she was right when she said you didn't need me to be your savior," she replied. I stared into her mesmerizing eyes quietly as I thought of that statement. Regardless of what she thought, I knew I couldn't have gotten to this point without Jarrah. She saved my life the moment she walked into my life at the playground. It may have taken some time for me to make a complete one-eighty, but I was on a long path to this change the moment Jarrah showed me something my mother had never shown me. Jarrah and Mama Charmaine's love was the only reason I had finally gotten here, and because of that, I had to see this through until I was a man, they both could be proud of.

Chapter 5: Where It Started

February 16, 2017
Brunson Park
Atlanta, Georgia

Spending time with Jarrah was exactly what I needed in my life after being without her for so long. If only I had gone to her in a civilized manner, we could have avoided the war I helped start out of pride. There were senseless casualties of that war of which I was still not proud. Although I didn't kill Summer myself, her blood was still on my hands. Even though I wasn't capable of giving her the love she desperately wanted from me, I could have kept her out of my bullshit. Because of me her and our child died in such a gruesome manner. Maybe if I had been in my right mind, I would have done better by her and that child. Not wanting to be the father to her baby was so fucked up on my part. After everything I went through with my own parents, I shouldn't have denied my only child just because I didn't create it with the woman, I wanted to have kids with. I realized it was a huge mistake on my part. I just wished I arrived at that realization when she broke the news to me. She warned me not to meet with Mama and Dario, but my faith in Mama led me to put her life in danger. The guilt had been gnawing at me as I sat in front of Jarrah, claiming to be a changed man. I had a lot of things I was keeping from her, but

I didn't exactly know how to come out and admit them. I knew I didn't have to tell Jarrah every part of my life. However, there was a part of me that wanted her to be proud of all of me, and not just the parts of me I revealed to her.

After breakfast, Jarrah and I drove to the place where it all began for us. As we pulled up to the park, I immediately began to reminisce on the day I met her for the first time. I remember looking into her big bright hazel eyes and being in awe of her. Aside from the bullshit I had to deal with from Monalisa, that was the best day of my life. My mother locked me out of the house so she could get high, so I went to the park as I usually did to get out of her hair for a while. However, she must have forgotten about me because I had been there all day, and she hadn't come for me like she usually did. It was late in the evening, so I had begun to cry because I thought Mona had forgotten about me. That's when Jarrah walked up to me, and tried to get me to tell her what was wrong with me. I was reluctant at first because I was embarrassed at myself and at my mother for putting me in the situation, but Jarrah never gave up on me. She sat quietly by me for at least an hour before I decided to tell her what was wrong. The other kids laughed at me, but she showed me compassion. That was something I would never forget.

After putting my Lincoln in park, and switching it off, I got out and hurried over to Jarrah's car so I could help her out of it. I watched her as she scanned the park through amazed eyes. I could tell she was reminiscing just like I was.

"Damn! The kids are lucky these days. When we were kids all we had was an old sliding board, some raggedy swings, and a merry go round that barely went around," she commented. I chuckled.

"You forgot about the rusty monkey bars and the sandless sandbox," I added, and she giggled.

"How could I forget about that?"

"I don't know how you could. I still have the blister on my hands to prove it," I joked as I eyed the palms of my hands. Jarrah looked at hers and we laughed in unison before we started toward the picnic tables. I grabbed the blanket she brought with her from her hands and placed it around her shoulders after unfolding it.

After I took my seat beside her, I looked at her, and asked, "You sure you're okay to sit out here? I don't want you to freeze."

"I'm okay. The winters here are nothing like Chicago's winters," she responded.

I sucked my teeth, and said, "Tell me about it." However, I could see she was in a daze, so I sat quietly and took in the moment with her.

"Do you remember the day we met," Jarrah asked me after a few minutes of silence.

"How could I forget it? It was the best and worst day of my life," I replied. She smiled.

"The irony of that is almost funny… I remember how angry I was at your mom for how she treated you that day."

"Yeah. That's something I could never forget. That was my whole life with that woman," I complained as I stared into space. I could see Jarrah look at me out the corner of my eye.

"Speaking of Monalisa, when was the last time you spoke to her," she asked me. I hesitated for a brief second.

"It's been a minute. I haven't actually spoken to her in at least a year, but I've responded to her texts whenever she would reach out for money. Aside from letting her know that I was going to Chicago, and… enlisting her in my bullshit revenge, I haven't really spoken to her for real."

"Does she know you're still alive," Jarrah questioned. I lowered my gaze.

"Quincy! Please tell me you don't have your mother still believing that you're dead?"

"What? I said I was working on myself, not that I had everything figured out."

"You're so full of shit," Jarrah laughed, and I joined her. She shook her head at me as I shrugged my shoulder. Fixing things with Monalisa was the last thing on my mind. Besides, I didn't have it like that to continue taking care of her like I had been doing, and I was only able to do that because of Jarrah. Once she left, I stopped helping my mother altogether.

"Honestly, I feel like I need to keep my distance from her until I'm in a better place," I admitted after our laughter died down.

"I get that, but... she isn't doing well since your death. We got into a fight at Mama's funeral. I may have attacked her out of anger," Jarrah confessed. I gasped dramatically and clutched my chest to taunt her. She playfully smacked my arm as we laughed like we did as children.

"You mean she got a taste of Jarrah Ali like I did that one time," I joked.

"Ugh! Shut up Q before I give you some more of Jarrah Ali," she threatened me as she balled her fists up at me. I held my hands up like she was holding me at gunpoint.

"I'm good on that. You got a mean left hook," I told her. She laughed hysterically. I stared at her as she giggled like a schoolgirl. I loved seeing her this way. When she was happy, I was at peace. It made me regret all the times I caused problems for her. I finally realized that by causing all of those problems for her, I was only hurting myself. Jarrah in her purest form was my peace and happiness, and I cheated myself out of that every time I hurt her. I was a fool like most men were in these situations. Why did I have to have this awakening when it was too late?

"I've heard that a time or two," she responded before she realized I was staring at her. I was so lost in thoughts of my regret I hadn't even heard what she said the first time, so she repeated herself.

"Q? Are you okay," she asked me. I snapped out of it and smiled at her to ease her mind.

"I'm good. Just got lost in thought for a minute," I admitted. She stared at me for a while before she slid closer to me and placed her head on my shoulder. I wrapped my left arm around her and held her close as I inhaled her scent. She always smelled like the fruit that grew on the trees on a tropical island. That alone was enough to disarm me. I don't know if she knew what I was feeling, but I was glad she was comfortable enough to get close to me.

"I don't know what's going on in that head of yours... but I want to remind you that you're not alone. It's okay if you are having regrets or whatever you're feeling, but you haven't completely lost me, Quincy," she assured me.

"Plus, you got your mother and your brother, who you need to mend things with as well," she added. I surrendered my gaze from her as I dealt with the shame of betraying Marcus. It was crazy that after yearning for a sibling for most of my childhood, I betrayed the only one I had when I should have embraced him. I doubted if Marcus was interested in reconciling with me after what I did to him.

"You make it sound so easy," I retorted as I fiddled with my fingers and gnawed on my inner cheek. Jarrah's soft warm hand palmed my cheek as she lifted my face toward hers.

"It's only as hard as you make it, Q. Marcus is a great person. I know he'd forgive you if you apologized to him, and Monalisa would be happy to know you're alive."

"Maybe, but I have to forgive myself for what I did first, especially to Marcus," I told her. If it were me, I would have never forgiven Marcus if he did what I did to him after just meeting him for the first time. I couldn't see past my thirst for vengeance, and it may have costed me my only brother.

Jarrah spellbound me with her beautiful hazel eyes before saying, "Rampage aside, you're still capable of being a good man, Quincy. You just have to see it in yourself. I still see it in you. The person I fell in love with is still inside of you," she reminded me. Then, she tilted her head toward my face. We stared at each other for a few seconds, and I couldn't help myself. I leaned down toward her and kissed her soft lips. I closed my eyes and relished the moment since she didn't stop me. I was surprised she was returning my kiss, but I tried not to think too deep about it. I knew this didn't mean I had a chance with her again, so for those few seconds, I exhaled and got caught in Jarrah's web. If she were a black widow, I would gladly be her prey. Nothing else mattered to me in that fleeting moment. After a few seconds, Jarrah broke away from me, buried her face in my chest, and squeezed me tight. I didn't know what was going on in her head, but I enjoyed the affection she was showing me.

"I still love you Jarrah and I don't know how to stop. I know I was awful to you in our marriage, and I don't deserve you at all... but I will always have these regrets if I don't try again. I know you are with the twins now, but I want to know if there's any sliver of hope for us," I asked her. Jarrah pulled away from me and looked me in my eyes for a few seconds like they did in romance movies.

"I love you, Q. I always will love you, but... I'm with the twins now. I'm sorry. I shouldn't have kissed you like that, but all of these feelings got me so confused," she answered. She didn't respond in the way I wanted her to, but she didn't completely shut me down either.

"There's something I need to tell you that I have been keeping from you all of this time," she confessed. My heart immediately sank into my stomach. I never thought she would keep something from me. I had been the one in our relationship with secrets. At least that's what I thought.

"Okay," I responded since I didn't know what else to say. Jarrah inhaled deeply and exhaled completely before adjusting herself on the picnic bench. If she was this nervous, then what she had to say had to be serious. That only put more fear in me. Jarrah was usually forthcoming with everything, even the things that were hard to say. Her communication skills were something I used to envy. I wished on many occasions that I had the strength, courage, and understanding to be as honest as she always was. So, if she was keeping a secret from me, that meant it had to be terrible. After the kiss we just shared, I expected things to get better for us, not worse. So, I prayed I could handle whatever this secret was. I could feel the pressure in my chest as I held my breath and waited for her to drop the atomic bomb, I knew this would be.

Chapter 6: The Final Goodbye

February 16, 2017
Brunson Lake
Atlanta, Georgia

By the look on Jarrah's face, I knew I needed to hold on to the edge of the picnic bench for this one. Her skin had turned slightly pale as she prepared to open up to me. I slid a few centimeters away from her, so I could turn to face her. My legs began to bounce uncontrollably as I anticipated what she was about to say. I could see her swallow the lump in her throat so whatever this was had been eating at her for a while. I squinted my eyes at her and studied her as my brain scrambled to figure out what it could be. I knew she had never cheated on me when we were together, so it couldn't be that. Also, it wouldn't make sense for her to confess something like that to me now. She didn't owe me anything as it pertained to that, especially since I cheated on her more times than I could remember, with more women than I could remember. So even if that were the case, I couldn't be mad at her. She had forgiven me numerous times, so I'd have to do the same if that were what she was keeping from me. However, something told me it was way worse than something as trivial as cheating.

Jarrah tucked piece of her coiled hair behind her ear, and breathed deeply again, before asking, "Do you remember that fight we got into when I found out you had given me a STD two years ago? The one you recently referenced when you called me Jarrah Ali?"

"Yeah. What about it," I inquired.

"Well, the reason I got so mad was because… I found out I miscarried because of the chlamydia you gave me, and it was the second time you caused me to lose our baby. The first time, I had been extremely stressed out from dealing with the debt you accumulated over a six-month span from gambling," she confessed. Suddenly, I felt like someone knocked the wind out of me. I couldn't believe what I was hearing. All of these years, I thought Jarrah couldn't get pregnant for me when she had been pregnant for me more than once and I caused her to lose our baby both times. That shit made me feel awful and I almost couldn't believe it.

"What?"

Jarrah dropped her head and chewed on her lips as I waited for her to clarify what she just exposed to me. "It wasn't that I couldn't get pregnant for you, but… the conditions I was living in while I was with you weren't healthy enough for a baby," she elaborated. I shook my head out of disbelief.

"Why did you keep that from me for so long?"

"I was trying to protect you. I didn't want you to punish yourself for it since it was what you wanted more than anything."

"So, you kept it to yourself and allowed me to punish you for it when it was my fault all along," I asked her rhetorically. I was baffled by this truth. It made me feel another level of hate for myself. I treated her like something was wrong with her when it was me that had the issues.

"Basically… and I'm only telling you now because I don't want any secrets between us this time around. I want us to start over, so… I felt like it was important for me to tell you everything. Please don't beat yourself up about this. It was wrong for me to keep it from you in the first place."

"I can't make that promise to you. You know I've wanted to have kids with you since we got married. I can't believe this. I just can't," I responded. Jarrah slid her arm through mine and leaned on my shoulder. She caressed my arm as we sat in silence for a while. Although I was reeling from the bomb she dropped on me, I decided I needed to be honest with her as well.

"I'm sorry, Quincy. I don't want you to feel bad. I've forgiven you, so I need you to forgive yourself," she told me. I massaged my temple for a few seconds as I gathered my thoughts. I wasn't expecting my meeting with Jarrah to go this way, but I had to be thankful she created this space for me to open up to her.

"That's hard, Jarrah. It's hard because… I did the shit again," I said. Jarrah sat erect and looked at me.

"What do you mean?"

I grabbed her hand and held onto it as I prepared myself to come clean. "Before Summer was killed… she told me that she was pregnant for me. I didn't want to accept her news because she wasn't you, so I denied that the child was mine. Had I known she was going to die because of me, I would have been okay with it because I didn't want to be the father to her child. I knew I divorced you because I was angry you couldn't give me the family I wanted, but even still, I couldn't see myself fathering anyone else's children. I denied her when all she wanted was my love and acceptance, and it cost her, her life. I'm an awful person for dragging her into my shit," I confessed as I shook my head.

"Shit! You are an awful person," Jarrah said before busting out in laughter. I turned my attention to her because I was caught off guard by her response.

"Jarrah?"

"Sorry, I couldn't help it. You're right. It's not funny," she teased as she wrestled with the bubble of laughter trying to escape her throat. I couldn't help but laugh at her. Our serious moment turned into a joke that fast. I thought she would be lecturing me, but she found it funny somehow.

"No, but seriously. I'm sorry for your loss... all of them," she joked as she tried to keep a straight face. I chuckled and shook my head at her.

"You ain't shit for that," I told her as I watched her laugh at my pain. At first, I was thrown off by it, but I realized why she took it as a joke. What other man could say he was a terrible father before he even got to have his children? Three of my children died before even being born because I was such an awful person. I didn't deserve to have kids of my own. That was a tough pill for me to swallow. Jarrah's laughter stopped when she realized I had gotten serious. I was quite sure she could read my mind because she slid her hand back in mine and kissed me on my cheek.

"Come on. Let's go say goodbye to Mama," she told me, before standing up. I followed her lead and walked beside her to the lake on the other side of Brunson Park. We made a lot of memories at the lake with Mama Charmaine. She taught us how to fish, swim, and took us camping on the campgrounds near the lake. It was a fitting place to spread her ashes since it was one of her favorite places. When we got to

Brunson Lake, Jarrah and I stood in front of it, and stared at the water as we had flashbacks of all the memories we shared with Mama. All of this was bizarre to me. Just three years ago, we were sitting around the kitchen table at Mama's house eating Sunday dinner. Now, we were having a memorial for her. I wished I had cherished them more when both of them were in my life. Maybe if I did, none of this would be happening. After Jarrah dialed Theresa's number and put her on speaker, we began our ceremony.

"I thought this would be the hardest part for me, but… since I'm standing here with you like she would have wanted, I'm at peace. I'm glad we could do this together," Jarrah acknowledged. I nodded my head to agree with her.

"So am I," Theresa said through the phone. Jarrah took the lid off the urn and poured some of Mama Charmaine's ashes into the lake.

"I'm going to miss you, Mama, but I'm finally at peace like you wanted me to be. Q, Terry, and I are going to keep your memory alive for as long as we live. We will come together to celebrate your life, and we will instill your memory in our children. You were such a great woman and an amazing mother… I love you so much, and I'm happy… I'm so happy that you're no longer suffering," Jarrah said through her tears. I placed my hand on the small of her back and rubbed her there to console her. She stepped back from the lake and handed me the urn, so I could say my peace.

I held the urn in my hand and stared at the ashes in the jar. It was so weird to me that a woman with a heart as big as Mama Charmaine's could fit in such a tiny jar. My tears began to fall from my eyes as I thought of my last moment with Mama. Although she allowed Dario to try to kill me, I could see in her eyes that she loved me until the very end. I wouldn't even be surprised if she had been praying the whole time that I would escape my fate that day. Once I got myself together, I stepped toward the lake and poured some of her ashes in there, and said, "Mama, I love you so much, and I'm thankful for the man you raised me to be. I'm sorry it took me so long to get my shit together. I wish you were here to witness it, but since you aren't… I have to thank you for raising a daughter who knows how to forgive. Regardless of our relationship, I promise to be the man I should have been all along for Jarrah's sake… I forgave you for what you did even before you done it. I knew you only wanted to protect Jarrah from me, but you don't have to worry about that anymore. With the second chance I got, I promise I'll dedicate it to protecting her for you. I'm gonna miss all of your words of wisdom and the kindness you've shown me since I came into your life. You meant so much to me because you loved me when my own mother couldn't. I will always love you for that, and you will always be my mama. Rest easy, Mama. You deserve to be at peace."

When I was done saying my goodbyes, Jarrah and I poured out the rest of Mama Charmaine's ashes on Theresa's behalf. Then, we held hands as we waited for Terry to say hers. "I can't believe you left me here to take care of these two by myself. You know I hold grudges, and you had the audacity to do the only thing that could bring Q and I back together again. I was not done hating him for being the asshole he is," Theresa joked. Jarrah and I laughed heartily through our tears. Leave it up to Theresa to make a sad moment funny.

"Anyways, on a serious note, I love you, Mama. You were the mother I needed desperately after my parents disowned me. If it weren't for you, I wouldn't have survived this long. I have tried to take my life on many occasions, and that was something I never shared with anyone, but I knew you knew. I could tell by the way you showed up for me each time I had done it. The random phone calls I received from you when I was feeling low weren't random at all. I know that now. Somehow, you knew I needed you in those moments. You were an angel God sent me when I couldn't love myself enough to live, so now I have to live for you. I promise you I will never give up on life again. I will fight every day. I love you so much Mama… and I'm going to miss you so much," Theresa said. The three of us shared a moment of silence after Terry was done with her speech. Mama Charmaine had been so important to the three of us, so this was a huge loss for us all. However, the only way to make her proud in death was to repair our relationship to what it had been before we were torn apart. Although I never cared for Theresa, she and I were close once, and I was glad to have her back in my life. Because of that, I would work hard to repair my relationship with her as well. Not just because it's what Mama Charmaine would have wanted, but because I wanted the three of us to be family again.

After we left Brunson Lake, Jarrah and I went back to my apartment. I expected her to go back to our childhood home with her new family, but she was determined to spend this entire day with me. That made me feel good, so I definitely wasn't complaining. I enjoyed her company very much. The thought of her leaving Atlanta again to go back to her new life with the twins made me sad, but I knew I needed to get out of her way and allow her to be happy. I didn't deserve her anyway, especially after hearing the secret she kept from me all of these years. Regardless of what she wanted; I couldn't help but hate myself for causing her to lose our children. The way I treated her when I thought she couldn't get pregnant for me was nothing less than despicable. I took my anger and frustration out on her every day because I couldn't understand why I couldn't create the legacy I wanted to create with her. Looking back, I now see that I had become so obsessed with getting her pregnant because I knew it was a sure way for her to stay with me. Having children with her was just another way for me to have power over her. Although I didn't act like it, I could tell she was getting fed up with me, so I wanted to lock her in forever so she wouldn't leave me. It was selfish as hell, but it was the truth, and that's why it didn't happen. God knew I was up to no good, so he stepped in.

"Hey! Where did you go, Q," Jarrah asked me as she looked into my eyes. We lied on my sectional and cuddled as we watched Woo, one of her favorite movies. After the ceremony, Jarrah asked if I wanted to eat snacks and watch movies like we used to do back in the day, and I was down because I wanted to spend as much time with her as I could before she left Atlanta for good. She must have asked me something about the movie, and because I was so deep in my head, I didn't hear her.

"My bad. I guess I was in my head. What did you ask me," I asked her. She stared at me for a while.

"Never mind. It's not important. Are you okay?"

"Yeah, I'm good," I lied. She studied me for a while through wise eyes. I knew she could see through me because she always did.

"You sure?" I nodded my head. I didn't want to ruin the moment we were having, so I decided to keep my thoughts to myself. I was enjoying this time with her even though I knew it was just a tease compared to what I wanted from her.

Jarrah kissed me on my cheek, and said, "I enjoyed this day with you, Quincy. I hope this isn't the last time I get to spend some alone time with you."

"Me either," I replied before kissing her on her forehead. She closed her eyes and held me close to her. Being this close to her made me horny as hell, but I tried to ignore it. Jarrah's scent, warm soft body, and energy was intoxicating to me. Just being near her made me crave her. I knew she could feel my erection on her ass, but she was doing an excellent job at ignoring it. I didn't want to make this moment about sex, so I internally told my dick to chill. I turned my attention back to the television to distract myself. The two of us cuddled and watched Woo until Jarrah fell asleep. I was sleepy too, but I didn't want to close my eyes and miss a single moment with her. I missed her so much when she was away, so it was hard for me to face the reality that this was just temporary. It took everything in me not to take her and leave the fucking country. A few days ago, I would have gone through with it, but I was really trying to be a better man. I gently kissed Jarrah on her shoulder. Then, I closed my eyes and inhaled her scent until I fell fast asleep.

Chapter 7: Manning Up

February 17, 2017
Highland Square Apartment Complex
Atlanta, Georgia

Boom, Boom, Boom, I heard as I fought to stay asleep. It sounded like someone dropped my unconscious body into a warzone, and I accepted my fate as a civilian out of his element since I wasn't ready to wake up and face the world again. My eyes opened abruptly as I remembered Jarrah was here with me. I immediately remembered the promise I made to Mama Charmaine at the homegoing ceremony Jarrah, Theresa and I had for her. I slowly scanned my living room as I gradually gained awareness. The pressure from Jarrah lying in my arms drew my attention to her. She was beautifully still asleep, and for a second, I got lost in her beauty, but that moment was ruined when I heard the sound again. Finally, my ears registered the unwarranted alarm as a knock on my apartment door. I slowly lifted Jarrah off of me and gently laid her back on the chair once I was free of the weight of her body. I glanced at her again to make sure I didn't disturb what looked to be a very peaceful sleep before I made my way to my door. No one knew where I had moved to except for Monalisa, Donald, and Jarrah. Monalisa still thought I was dead, so I knew it wasn't her, which meant it could only be one person.

As I peeped through my peephole and confirmed Donald's identity, I breathed deeply as I decided how I would handle him. Before I opened the door for him, I walked back into my living room and retrieved my cell phone from my coffee table. I found Dario's number in my contacts and shot him a quick text message.

Come to my apartment ASAP. We might have a problem.

Shoot me the location.

1400 Briarcliff Rd. Atlanta, GA 30306 Apt. 83G. I'm on the 8th floor.

OMW.

It's gated so use my pin 184730 to get in.

Word. After I read Dario's last text message, I put my phone back on the table and went back to the door. I took a deep breath before I unlocked the door and twisted the doorknob. I hadn't seen Donald in a few days, so I didn't know what he was on. The last conversation we had didn't go well since he was angry at me for ruining our plans since I gave Jarrah my word that I would drop my vendetta against the twins. He disappeared for a while, and it slipped my mind to alert the security at my apartment complex not to allow him back inside. I should have done that and changed my PIN, but I was so caught up in getting my life together that I forgot. He had shown up at my door unannounced, and I didn't know what to expect. That's why I hit Dario up before I opened the door for Donald. If something popped off, I didn't want Jarrah to be caught in the crossfire. Finally, I opened the door so Donald could stop knocking. It was almost midnight, and he was going to get me reported for disturbing the peace if he didn't chill out. Plus, I didn't want him to wake Jarrah because I didn't want him to know she was here, for her safety. I also didn't want her to see he still had access to me. I worked hard to get her to trust me again, so I wasn't planning to break it.

"What's up," Donald greeted me once we were face to face. I stood in front of the door so he wouldn't walk inside my place like he usually did.

"What's up? I thought you went back to Indiana," I told him. He grinned at me.

"There's no way I could leave without saying goodbye to my partner in crime," he teased. I looked at him stone-faced and unamused. He was a pest to me, and I regretted I dealt with him in the first place. However, he saved my life, so I felt like I was indebted to him.

"Is that why you're here? To say goodbye," I inquired because I knew better than that. He smirked at me, and it gave me chills. There was something more sinister about his energy this time.

"Something like that," he responded.

"So… aren't you going to let me in?"

I sighed deeply before stepping back and allowing him to come into my apartment. Before he could make his way to my living room, I redirected him to my dining area, so he wouldn't see Jarrah on my couch. Once we were in there, I walked to the bar and poured the two of us a shot of whiskey. I needed to get some liquor in his system so I could be at an advantage if things popped off. I only lived about ten minutes from Mama Charmaine's house, so I knew Dario would be here soon. However, I didn't want to take any chances. I handed Donald his drink and stared at him as I waited for him to drink it. He kept his eyes on me like he knew I was up to no good, but he took the shot after a few seconds. I threw mine back right after him and poured us another one.

"So, what's up? Why'd you come here so late," I questioned as I nursed my second shot. I wasn't lightweight, but I wanted him to take a couple before I drank another one.

After Donald threw back two more shots, he looked at me, and said, "In case you've forgotten, I ain't from here, so I don't have a place to go."

"Then, where have you been for the past few days," I questioned. He glared at me.

"Aren't you going to drink that? I'm five shots in and you haven't even touched your second one," he pointed out, dodging my question. I took my second shot, so he could shut up about it. He poured me another one after taking another one. I knew alcohol was his weakness, so he wouldn't hesitate to fill up on it if I offered him a drink. Although I knew he wasn't stupid, I knew he couldn't resist the urge to get drunk since that was his favorite pastime. If you looked up the word alcoholic in Webster's dictionary, there would be a picture of him wearing a sombrero and holding up a bottle of tequila with a lime in his mouth.

I drank my third shot and winced as it burned the back of my throat. I hated the sting of alcohol, but I drank it anyway. I wasn't an alcoholic like Donald, but I had a love-hate relationship with the bottle of spirits. I had seen my mother lose herself in bottle after bottle when I was a little boy, so I loathed it, but not enough to not drink it at all. Donald slid the bottle over to me so I could pour my fourth shot, and I immediately slid it back over to him. "Nah, I'm good. You gone answer my question or what?"

"I went to see some distant relatives of mine," he lied. I knew he was lying because I knew he didn't know anyone here. His family was from Indiana, and they all remained together since they were in the Mexican Mafia. Summer told me how obsessed her father was with keeping the family together during pillow top. That's why he sent Donald after her when she flew to Chicago to help me out. It was like they had a tracker on her, and she desperately wanted to escape their stronghold. Fucking with me got her what she wanted permanently. That was the one thing I regretted out of this whole ordeal. I shouldn't have included her in my bullshit. I knew she was in love with me. She would have done anything for me, and I used that to manipulate her. That was fucked up on my part.

"That's the story you gone spin to me," I quizzed as I stared at him. He laughed loudly. I slowly turned my head toward my living room, afraid that he would wake Jarrah. He must have noticed my paranoia because his laughter abruptly stopped.

"Is someone else here with you," he asked me. I quickly turned my attention back to him.

"No. What would make you think that?"

He studied me for a while before saying, "You've been acting a little suspicious since I came here. Questioning me and shit like you don't owe me for saving your fuckin' life. So, it would make sense if you were hiding something from me. Are you... hiding something from me, Quincy," he inquired. His crazed eyes glistened as we stared at each other. I tried to keep my cool even though I was worried about what would happen if he found out Jarrah was here.

"I don't got shit to hide," I answered as I poured another shot.

"Oh really? Then, why are we sitting at this uncomfortable ass table instead of the living room like we usually do? You got a lady friend in there waiting on you," he pressed through a creepy smile. I rolled my eyes and sighed deeply.

"I said no. Besides, if anyone is acting suspicious it's you. Talking about you went to see family when I know full well you don't have family here. I'm not stupid nigga."

"Nigga? *¿Me parezco una nigger para ti*? The only nigger sitting at this table is your black ass," he spat in the most condescending tone I'd ever heard. His racist ass was sitting here acting like he wasn't half-black. Just because his skin was lighter than mine, didn't mean he wasn't a black man. You would have thought he was raised by a slave master the way he hated the black in himself.

"If you call me a nigger again, I will-" I started to say, but before I could finish my statement, Donald stood up like he wanted to fight me, so I stood up too. I may not have come from the background he came from, but I was going to defend myself when I was disrespected. I didn't care that he was in a gang. Nothing about him scared me. We stood up and glared at each other from opposite sides of my dining room table, and waited to see who would make the first move. Suddenly, Jarrah's voice permeated my apartment like an alarm.

"Quincy," she called out to me as my chest heaved. Donald frowned at me as he processed Jarrah's voice. Before he could make a move, there was a knock at my door. A sense of relief came over me as I tried to decide what I would do first. Jarrah was looking for me, so I knew it was a matter of time before she got up and started walking around my apartment to find me. However, Dario had finally arrived to pick her up. I didn't want her to know Donald was still around, so I quickly walked to my door and opened it for Dario. I was glad to see that he brought Dustin and Deandra's husband with him.

"She's in the living room. Go take care of her while I handle things in here. I don't want her to know Donald's here," I explained to Dario. He nodded at me and walked to my living room. Dustin followed him while Jerrell followed me to my dining room.

"What are you guys doing here? Where's Q," I heard Jarrah ask the twins. I hated that this situation escalated to the point that I had to ask Thing One and Thing Two for help. I may have squashed my beef with them, but I still didn't care for them. Donald was sitting down when I got back in my dining room. He must have seen the twins pass by and realized he was outnumbered. He grabbed the bottle of whiskey and took another shot. Then, he stood up and started out of my apartment.

When he got closer to my front door, he turned to look at me before saying, "My business with you isn't finished in the slightest. You owe me, and I'll be back to collect when your posse ain't around." Then, he walked out of my apartment. Upon hearing those words, Jerrell started to my living room, and I followed behind him. I was glad they arrived before things got ugly. The last thing I wanted was for Jarrah to get hurt because of me. Donald was on one from the minute he arrived at my apartment, that's why I didn't take any chances with him. When I got in my living room, Dario was putting Jarrah's shoes on, and Dustin was helping her put on her jacket while Jerrell gathered her things. It was weird watching them wait on her like she was a queen, but I couldn't be mad at it. I hadn't done any of those things for her, ever. As strange as they were to me, I couldn't help but be happy she had people who loved her the way they clearly did. Even Deandra's husband loved her. I could tell because he made sure Donald wasn't a risk to her before he went to see her. She had all of them eating out of the palms of her hands, and I was low-key amazed at her for it. As crazy as it was, it made me love her more.

"There you are, Q. What happened? Where did you go," she asked me all at once. I stared at her as I tried to figure out how to cover my ass, but I was at a loss for words. Donald's threat was getting to me.

"Nothing happened. It was late so we came looking for you. Quincy was just letting us in when you woke up," Dario told her, covering for me. Jarrah stared at me to see if his story checked out. I smiled at her so she would know I was okay. It meant a lot to see she still cared about me. It also meant a lot that Dario covered for me without me asking him to. He could have told her I was still dealing with Donald, so she wouldn't want to deal with me anymore, but he didn't. I had nothing but respect for him for that.

"I guess they thought I was going to steal you again," I joked. The twins and Jerrell turned toward me abruptly, and things suddenly became awkward.

"Too soon," I asked sarcastically. Jarrah giggled as she walked toward me. The rest of them didn't find the humor in my joke. I was quite sure they felt the same way I felt about them, and I was okay with that. Repairing my relationship with Jarrah didn't mean I had to be friends with them. I wanted no parts of the weird ass reverse harem Jarrah had created with them. I wanted her to love me and only me. I may have been changing, but I was still selfish as fuck when it came to her.

"Hey, can you guys give me a minute with him? I'll be out soon," she told them.

"We'll wait for you outside the apartment. I'm not comfortable letting you walk to the car by yourself," Dario responded to her as he eyed me. I knew that was his way of saying he didn't trust me, and I couldn't fault him for that. The fact that Donald still had access to me was bad for my relationship with Jarrah. I knew I needed to cut ties with him since he wasn't happy, we squashed everything, but I couldn't help but feel indebted to him. The three of them left my apartment, so Jarrah could say her goodbyes to me. I sat on the arm of my chair as I shook my head at Jarrah. She must have known what I was thinking because she smiled.

"Don't you even start," she warned me before I could say anything. I chuckled.

"It must be nice to have them niggas wrapped around your fingers like that. They treat you like you're Queen Elizabeth or something," I teased. Jarrah laughed.

"Are you jealous?"

"Hell yeah, I'm jealous. I want you all to myself, though. I ain't interested in that sharing shit," I told her. She shook her head at me.

"Anyways… I enjoyed myself with you today. It was nice to see this side of you," she confessed. I stared into her big doe eyes and got lost in them for a few seconds.

"I enjoyed myself too. I wish we could do this every day, but I see you got your hands full," I joked. Jarrah playfully smacked my leg as we laughed heartily.

"You're not funny Q. You get on my nerves," she giggled. I reached out and pulled her into me and held her tight. She laid her head on my chest and listened to my heartbeat. For a while, we stood in silence.

"I'm so glad you're alive, Quincy."

"Me too."

"Keep it that way. Stay out of trouble so you can keep your promise to Mama," she told me. I could tell she knew something was up. My situation with Donald wasn't resolved, so my life was in danger until it was. He was angry at me for not keeping my word, and a part of me understood why. I owed him so much for saving my life. I just didn't want to pay him the way he wanted me to. I loved Jarrah, so I couldn't take Dario away from her like Donald wanted me to. I wanted her to be happy, even if it weren't with me.

"I'm gonna miss you so much," I admitted before kissing her temple. She squeezed my waist tight and tilted her head toward me. I bowed my head to meet her halfway for one last kiss. She tipped-toed and kissed me softly. I exhaled as I tasted her sweet lips. I wanted so bad to rewind time. I wanted to go back and be the man she needed from the moment I decided I wanted her to be my forever. I hated that I was too inadequate to love her the way she deserved to be loved. I had to accept that loving her meant making the best decision for her, and although I hated to admit it, the twins were better men for her than I was. I could tell they loved her unconditionally. That was something I failed to do when we were together, so I had to pay the price for it. Jarrah pulled away from me, and it took everything in me not to devour her.

"Promise me that you won't forget about me, Jarrah," I asked her. She flashed me a genial smile.

"I couldn't forget about you if I tried, Quincy Travante Carter," she responded. I adorned her with a forehead kiss.

"I'll never stop loving you, Jarrah."

"I know you won't. I will always love you too. I need you to promise me that you will move on. You deserve to be happy too. You deserve to be loved. Let somebody other than me love you, Quincy. You deserve it just as much as I do... Also, go see your mother and fix things with Marcus and her. It's not too late," she told me. I nodded at her. It was going to be hard to live without her, but I knew she was right about everything she said.

"You know you can call me whenever you need me. My-"

"Number will always be the same," Jarrah grinned, finishing my sentence. I chuckled at her for teasing me for recycling old lines. She stroked my cheek and stared at me for a few seconds.

"Walk me to the door," she commanded as she interlocked her fingers in mine. My feet felt heavy as we neared my front door. It was like my body was rejecting the idea of being without her.

Once we were there, Jarrah twisted the knob, and turned back to look at me. "Goodbye Quincy! Take care of yourself," she told me before pulling the door open, and walking out of it. I stood in the doorway and watched as she walked away with the twins and Jerrell. I may have been reluctant to let her go, but I knew that being with them was what was best for her. She deserved the type of people that were willing to go to war for her. We made a promise that we would keep our little family together, so this wasn't goodbye forever. I knew I would see her again. In the meantime, I needed to get my life together, and become the man she saw in me from the beginning. First, I'd deal with Donald so I wouldn't have to look over my shoulder. After our business was resolved, I would take Jarrah's advice and allow myself to be loved again. I may have done some terrible things in my life, but it wasn't too late to turn things around for myself. After spending time with her, I was reminded of the potential that lay dormant inside me. I killed the part of me that self-sabotaged out of fear, so now it was about time for a rebirth.

Chapter 8: A New Thrill

February 17, 2017
Dave's Bar & Grill
Atlanta, Georgia

After leaving my hotel, The Carter, I drove over to Dave's Bar & Grill for a meeting. Last night's debacle with Donald left a bad taste in my mouth. However, I had to put it behind me to get back on my businessman shit. I was determined to rebuild my wealth and I knew the best way to do that was to expand. I had three hotels in Atlanta already, but it was time for me to take my franchise out of state. Atlanta was a strong start, but I wanted my franchise to reach various parts of the country, and if I were successful enough, I'd build one overseas. Jarrah not being around may have made me uncomfortable, but it didn't discourage my ambition. I was ambitious before I met her. She was just the battery in my back that kept me motivated and on track. Handling my business myself was a lot of responsibility, but I would get used to it in time. I still had to hire a new assistant since I got rid of Kiandra's ridiculous ass. After dealing with her bullshit, I had been a little nervous about bringing someone else in. It was scary as hell to think of the things people would do to take you down when they weren't happy with the way you handled things with them. I was a successful black man in America, so I always had to be weary of enemies. People would do and say anything to fuck things up for me when I wouldn't bend to their will. I learned my lesson for sure, so I knew not to mix business with pleasure again.

As I sat at my table in the bar and waited for my guests to arrive, I thought about what I would do to handle the Donald situation. I couldn't pay him off since I didn't have the kind of money that would get him off my back for good, so money was out of the question. I was starting from nothing, so I needed to build my nest egg back up before I could do shit like that again. Donald was after blood for his sister's murder, so money wouldn't have been enough anyway. He was dealing with being ostracized from his family since his sister got killed under his watch, so he was desperate for a way to get back in his father's good graces. A light bulb went off in my head as I thought things over. If I could get Donald to go for it, then I may have found my solution to the problem. After the day I spent with Jarrah yesterday, there was no way I was going to insert myself back into that drama. Getting her to forgive me was a dream come true. Besides, I had bigger things to worry about than something as petty as some revenge. I was on a mission to gain my wealth back, so I needed to focus on my businesses.

As I checked the time on my cell phone, I could feel someone looking at me. I stopped in my tracks and slowly turned my attention to Aurora, who was staring at me from a few tables over. She was looking at me like she wanted to ravage me in the middle of the bar. I nodded my head at her and flashed her a devious smile. Her eyes pervaded my mind, and suddenly I was hypnotized. She was fine as hell in the teal blue bodycon dress she was wearing. I had been staring so hard I didn't realize she was sitting in front of a man whose back was facing me. I assumed he was her husband, and I immediately understood why she had been throwing her pussy at me like she was Tom Brady. The man she was sitting with was a short chubby white man who looked like he played video games in his mother's basement and hacked into beautiful women's camera phones to spy on them. She was too beautiful to be with a man like that which made me assume he was rich. I could have been wrong, but I doubted it. Women who looked like her only dated men like that if they had much to gain. The man was so focused on chasing his peas around his plate he hadn't even noticed Aurora eye fucking me. I dodged her advances the first time, but since I saw what she had to go home to every night, I almost felt bad enough to put this dick in her.

For a second, she turned her attention to what I assumed was her phone in her lap. I averted my eyes from her so I wouldn't seem like a creep. That's when my cell phone went off. I unlocked it and saw a message from her. Before I opened it, I glanced at her to see if she was watching me, and she was.

You in the mood for dessert? A broad smile painted my face as I eyed her message. I was shocked at how hard she came at me, but I couldn't deny my interest in her. Before I responded, I looked in her direction again, but this time she was gone, so I assumed she went to the ladies' room. I immediately got excited about what was about to go down if I played my cards right, so I tapped my screen to respond.

That depends. You offering to treat me? As I eyed the dots on my screen and waited for her to respond, I fantasized about all the things I wanted to do to her. My fantasy was interrupted by a video of her playing with her neatly manicured pussy in the bathroom. My dick immediately hardened, and suddenly the lessons I learned from the bullshit I went through with Kiandra went out the window. Aurora was sexy as fuck, so it was hard for me to fight the temptation.

You're such a tease.

I'm not teasing you baby. That was an invitation.

Oh really? You sure your husband won't mind?

What he doesn't know won't hurt him. You coming or what? My leg bounced as I tried to decide if I was going to tow the lines between business and pleasure again. What Kiandra tried to do to me should have been enough to deter me, but I was still a man who was overdue for some new pussy. That short relationship I had with Deandra when we were working together in Chicago was just an appetizer. I was ready for the full-course meal and Aurora looked like she did the body good like soul food. Jarrah did encourage me to move on, and even though this was not what she meant, it was what was available to me. I stood up out of my seat and walked over to the hostess to inform her to let my party know I was running to the bathroom for a minute if they came before I was done with Aurora. They had been late to our meeting anyway, so I was okay with making them wait for me for a while. I had a beautiful Blasian goddess waiting for me in the ladies' room, so I couldn't waste any time.

When I approached the ladies' room, I knocked on the door and waited for a response before I opened it. Aurora immediately opened the door for me with an innocent look on her face. It was ironic how the most innocent-looking women usually were the most devilish ones. I should have been weary of fucking a married woman while her husband was in the vicinity, but lust had overcome me the moment I saw her staring at me from across the restaurant. I looked around to make sure no one saw me come to the ladies' room. Then, I walked in. Aurora stepped back slowly as she gazed into my eyes. I kept my eyes on her as I stood in front of her. She brought her panties from behind her and dangled them in my face like I was a wild bull she was taunting. I stepped closer to her, grabbed her by her neck, and pressed her into the door. She locked the door as I lifted her a bit and held her in place so I could give her a quickie. I liked the thrill of fucking her while her husband was in the building, but I didn't want to take the chance of him coming to look for her, so I knew I had to make it quick. Although I wanted to put my dick in her throat first, I knew I didn't have time for that.

"You sure you wanna do this," I asked her to make sure I was getting her consent. I didn't want a repeat of what happened with Kiandra.

"I've never been so sure in my life," she responded. What she said turned me on so much my dick jump. I loved it when a woman was feigning for me like I was crack. As I pinned her against the door with my left hand. I undid my pants with my right hand. As soon as my dick was free, I slid a condom on it and penetrated her pussy. I exhaled hard as her walls encased my dick. Her shit was tight and wet, it almost felt like I was in her raw. I began stroking her slowly at first, so my dick could get used to being in new pussy. My shit could be shy sometimes, so I hoped it stayed hard without the warmup I usually needed.

"I know that's not all you got, Mr. Carter. Fuck me like you mean it," Aurora commanded. She caught me by surprise with what she said, but my dick had been excited to give her what she wanted. I sped up my pace like I put my shit in second gear. Aurora tongued me down, so she must have liked what I was giving her. It boosted my ego a bit, so I plunged into her deeper and with more force.

"Hell yeah! That's it, baby. Keep it right there," she praised. I kept the rhythm I was at as I fondled her small breasts through her dress. She pulled her straps down and freed them, so I could stimulate them with my tongue. I didn't hesitate to suck on her light brown nipples.

"Fuck," I groaned as I pumped into her wetness. Even through the condom I was wearing, she felt good as hell. I was almost at climax, but I prayed my dick didn't give out on me too soon. I knew this was a quickie, but I didn't want it to be over just yet. Aurora held onto my neck as she bounced on my dick. I stepped back from the door slowly, so she could go to work. She rode me like this was a rodeo, and she was trying to win the prize. It took so much out of me not to bust all in her good-ass pussy. I held onto her waist and assisted her.

"Oooo, fuck! I'm about to cum," she whined in a low tone. A part of me was happy because I was ready to erupt, but I didn't want to stop. I was used to going a few rounds while having sex, so quickies weren't my thing. However, I was happy to get what I could after not having sex for over a week. Deandra was the last person I slept with, and although she was unhinged, she had some amazing pussy. However, Aurora had something more that made me crave her even while I was inside her. It was dangerous as hell for me to feel like that, but I liked the thrill of it all. After a couple of minutes, I could feel her walls pulsate around my dick while she became more slippery.

"Aaaah," she sang as she creamed on my manhood. I dug into her deeper before ejaculating. I stayed inside her and pressed her back into the door. Then, I kissed her lips and moved down to her neck, shoulder, and then her breasts.

"I want you. I want you to be mine," I unintentionally whispered to her. I immediately felt embarrassed by what I said. For a while, she was silent, which made me nervous. Then, she winded her hips on me as she sucked on my tongue.

"You're so fuckin' intoxicating, Mr. Carter. I want you too," she admitted. I stared at her for a while, and she seemed sincere. I licked my thumb and stimulated her clit as I pumped into her again. I deeply stroked her as I kept my eyes on her innocent eyes. It was crazy to me how she could keep her innocence while being freaky. It reminded me of Jarrah. I didn't know if I was tripping because I didn't want to be alone, but I started to feel something for her.

"I don't give a fuck about your husband. You're mine now," I stated, surprising myself.

"Oh yeah? Then, show me."

I pulled out of Aurora and let her down. She turned facing the door, placed her hands on it, and arched her back so I could enter her from behind. I slid my used condom off, put on a new one, and slid my dick back in her. I pushed it as deep as it could go inside her. I smacked her petite ass and held on to her waist as I gave her dick that I had never given anyone before. She moaned softly so she wouldn't give us away. I plowed into her like I had something to lose if I didn't fuck her properly. I wanted to experience her again, so I had to make a good impression on her if I wanted to have access to this good pussy.

"Mmmm, you feel so good inside me Quincy," she moaned as I penetrated her sensitive walls. I pumped into her and stirred my dick in her thoroughly as I smacked her ass in between.

"God damn this pussy is so good," I grunted. Aurora looked back at me and smirked. Immediately, I was caught in her trance, and suddenly I was busting another load inside her. She orgasmed after me. I reluctantly pulled out of her and stood up to get myself together. I didn't want it to be over, but we had been in the bathroom for at least ten minutes. It was a matter of time before her husband came looking for her. Aurora cleaned herself up and fixed her clothes in silence. I hoped the things she said to me weren't just a show for sex. I shouldn't have cared since she was married, but I couldn't help myself. I wanted her badly. I stood and watched her as I waited for her to give me confirmation that this wasn't a one-time thing. I didn't have the balls to ask her myself because I didn't want to get rejected.

"I should leave before you since I've been here longer. I'm sure he's wondering where I've been... If he even notices I've been gone at all," she told me through gloomy eyes like she dreaded going back to her husband. I couldn't help but want to save her from her misery.

"Well, he's an idiot if he doesn't notice. If I were your man, I wouldn't let you out of my eyesight," I assured her. She looked at me and smiled. Then, she walked over to me.

"I knew I was right about you, Mr. Carter," she said as she wrapped her arms around my neck and anchored her eyes on me while I held her close to me.

"You know you can call me Quincy right, especially considering what we just did," I told her. It was weird that she kept calling me Mr. Carter like I was her elder. She looked young, but I assumed she was at least in her late twenties. I hoped I was right. I wasn't into young women. I was not my father's son in that way.

"I like Mr. Carter better. It's sexy to me," she clarified. I could tell she was good with her words and was used to people allowing her to say and do as she pleased. She knew what to say to get me where she wanted me, and I was too weak to counter it. Aurora kissed my lips again, for a few seconds. After that, she pulled away from me.

"This was fun. I'd like to do it again some time," she finally said. My dick jumped at the thought of being buried deep within her, and just like that, I was on her hook. I knew stepping into this with her was risky in many ways, but I was willing to take the risk. It had been a while since I was this interested in a woman who wasn't Jarrah. If I played my cards right, she could be the next Mrs. Carter. It may have been naïve of me to think I could take a married woman from her husband, but I was up for the challenge. I felt like Aurora was worth it. She had all the things that attracted me to a woman – beauty, brains, and body. So, she was a great catch in my eyes. After she kissed me goodbye, she left the bathroom. I stayed back for a few minutes, so no one would see us leaving behind each other. Then, when I thought the coast was clear, I exited the bathroom. It had been a coincidence that I ran into Aurora at the bar, but I was glad it happened. I didn't know if fate was playing with my life or what, but this encounter felt like it was supposed to happen. I hoped I was right, and I wasn't just making excuses to be impulsive like I usually was. Dealing with a woman who was contractually obligated to another man was normally not my type of trouble to get into, but for Aurora, I'd set aside my principles just this once.

Chapter 9: Strictly Business

February 17, 2017
Dave's Bar & Grill
Atlanta, Georgia

As I made my way back inside the bar, I noticed an increase in the number of people since I first came. I immediately looked at Aurora's table to see if she was still there, but her husband and she were gone. I wondered if I were the only man, she was having an affair with. I knew she wasn't actually mine, but I would feel some type of way if she were having sex with someone other than me. I wanted to be her one and only, but I knew I had to get her husband out of the way first. I was willing to do whatever it took to get what I wanted. I had always been this way. It got me into trouble sometimes, but there was nothing wrong with a little trouble here and there. I knew I should have slowed my role after everything I had been through with Kiandra, but I couldn't help myself. I couldn't deny that a part of me loved drama. It was thrilling to walk on the wild side, and I may have enjoyed it entirely too much. I could see Jarrah shaking her head at me right now if she knew what I was up to.

When I arrived at my table, I was shocked to see that my party had arrived. A part of me doubted they would see me after everything I put them through. They didn't look so happy with me since I had them waiting, but I was thankful they still came to have this meeting with me. I was serious about wanting to expand my business, so I knew I had to prove myself for them to trust me. Once I sat down, the three of us sat in silence for at least a minute as we stared at each other. I was a little nervous because I was coming back to them for help after I gave them hell the last time we worked together. I allowed my jealousy and ego to get the best of me when I came at them with that lawsuit I filed under false pretenses. They had every right to refuse to do business with me ever again and I couldn't even be upset about it. I exhaled deeply as I got ready to do something I would have never done before this little awakening I had. I hoped I was able to get my intentions through to them in this conversation. They eyed me sternly as they waited for me to tell them why I called them to the bar. I adjusted myself in my seat and cleared my throat as I prepared to plead my case.

"Thanks for coming to meet with me after everything I've done to make your lives hell. I know I don't deserve a second chance from you, but I appreciate you for at least hearing me out," I stated, attempting to slice through the awkward silence between us.

"You know Jarrah is the only reason we're here, so don't think for a second that we're happy about this," Dario frowned. I nodded.

"I know, but I'm still thankful," I reiterated. Dario sighed deeply and leaned forward with his hands placed on the table.

"Why did you call us here, Quincy," Dustin asked me. I lowered my gaze and tried to find my words.

"Well, I wanted to talk to you about the development of my hotel," I said. Dario winced. I could tell he was still bitter from our dealings with each other concerning my hotel.

"Your hotel? Last time I checked, you weren't happy with how things were going with *your* hotel," Dario commented. I shook my head.

"I know. I was just being an asshole, and I apologize for that. I was just upset that you were with Jarrah, so I made some stupid decisions."

"You think," Dustin said as he shook his head. I knew they weren't feeling me, but I needed them more than I wanted to admit.

"Look... it's hard for me to come here and basically beg you to help me out, but... I'm desperate as hell. I know you know shit hasn't been going well for me, and I'm not looking for sympathy. I just want to extend the olive branch, so we can be cordial, and do business together. That's it. I promise there won't be any more problems or tricks from me. I'm done with revenge. I just want to move forward with my life," I elaborated. They sat in silence and stared at me. I poured my heart out to them, so I hoped they could let bygones be bygones and give me another chance. Dustin dug into his pocket and pulled something out of it. Then, he handed it to me. I grabbed the sheet of paper from him and opened it up. I was shocked at what I saw.

"What is this?"

"It's a check for six million dollars. Jarrah told us to give it to you. She said she knew you wouldn't accept it from her, so she gave it to us," Dustin explained. I kept my eyes on the check. I couldn't believe Jarrah would do this for me. I was upset when she got half of my money during the divorce when I should have been thankful. She deserved all of it, so it would have been hard for me to take it back from her, but I wasn't going to allow my pride to keep me from accepting it when I knew I needed it.

"Why would she do this for me after everything I've done to her," I asked rhetorically.

"Because that's who she is. You should know that better than anyone. Although you don't deserve it, don't worry about it. She's good forever. We got more than enough to take care of her," Dario declared. I knew it was his way of telling me they were better equipped to take care of her. I was crawling on my knees to beg for their help, and she had done this for me. He was right, though. I didn't deserve any of this, but I was so happy for it that I could cry.

"Besides, you're going to need it if you want me to finish your hotel because my price just went up," Dustin stated. I looked at him with bright eyes. I knew they were doing this for Jarrah, but I was still thankful.

"Thank you, man! I promise you I won't get in your way this time," I vowed. Dustin nodded at me.

"Thank Jarrah. I'm only doing this for her. I know you're important to her, and although I don't care for you, I wouldn't do anything that would hurt her."

"As long as you stay out of my way, we can work together again. You already know how I feel about you. My brother is more forgiving, but I'm still keeping my eyes on you," Dario warned me. If he knew what I shared with Jarrah yesterday, he would have killed me for real this time, but I damn sure wasn't going to say anything. Jarrah may have moved on with them, but she would always have a place with me if she wanted it. I'd stay away from her to keep the drama down, but if she wanted me back, I wasn't going to turn her down.

"I don't want any more problems with you. All I want is to do business with you," I told them.

"Good. Keep it that way. I'm not befriending another nigga for Jarrah's sake. This is strictly business," Dario said. I couldn't help but chuckle at him. Jarrah was forcing them to reconcile their differences with everyone. She had always been that way. She had this obsession with resolving conflicts and befriending everyone like she was Jesus or something.

"Jarrah can be a handful, but… she really cares about people. That's why she's so big on reconciliation. Her father died after having a fight with her mother, so she hates the thought of leaving things unresolved. I know I don't have to tell you this, but… please take care of her. She overextends herself, without a thought about her own wellbeing. She won't admit when she needs help or support. You gotta learn her so you can tell when she needs you the most," I explained to them. I may not have cared for them, but I wanted them to treat Jarrah right because she deserved it.

"Don't worry, we know how she can be. There's nothing we wouldn't do for her," Dustin retorted. I could tell he meant that with his soul. I was happy for her for finding people that could love, support, and treat her like the queen she was. I made a mistake by letting her go, but that mistake led her to them, so I couldn't be too mad about it.

"Yeah, we got her," Dario added. I shook my head at them. We sat in silence for a while and stared at each other. It was funny to me how things turned out. A few weeks ago, we had been battling for Jarrah's affections. Now, we were sitting around the table influenced by her to put the past behind us. Jarrah was amazing to be capable of making us call a truce. The power she had over the three of us was unbelievable.

"I'll draw up new contracts when we get back to Chicago, and I'll hit you up when I'm done," Dario told me.

"Okay cool."

"One more thing I want to ask you," Dustin announced. I gave him my attention and waited for him to ask me what he needed to ask.

"What's your relationship with Summer's brother?"

I knew eventually they were going to bring up Donald because of last night's debacle. "I don't have a relationship with him. He saved my life, so he feels like I owe him. Don't worry though. I'm going to handle him for good, so Jarrah will be safe," I swore to them.

"You better. She's been through enough already thanks to you," Dario spat.

"You mean thanks to all of us," Dustin chimed in. I was glad one of them was taking responsibility for the part they played in Jarrah's misery. While I did betray her, I didn't play a huge role in the war until Dario tried to kill me. If that never happened, things wouldn't have been as bad as they were.

"Anyways, if we're done here, we can part ways," Dario said. At first, I thought he was trying to get away from me as fast as he could, but since he had been eyeing his phone occasionally throughout our conversation, I figured something else had his attention. Since Jerrell wasn't with them, I assumed he was with Jarrah. That was why he was rushing to leave the bar.

"Go ahead. I'm about to get some food since I'm not in the mood for whatever Anna is cooking tonight," Dustin told him. Dario sucked his teeth.

"You don't even know what she's cooking tonight."

"I know it's going to be some Dominican dish I don't want. That's all I need to know," Dustin countered as he looked at the menu. It was interesting seeing them interact with each other. I wondered how Jarrah dealt with it. I looked around for the waitress and called her over to the table.

"Why don't y'all let me treat you to a meal," I offered. The twins both eyed me like I was tripping.

"No offense, but you need to keep every dime you got in your pocket," Dario said. Dustin chuckled. What he said didn't bother me like it would have before. Although the millions of dollars they had didn't compare to my little six million, I was still grateful. So, I was able to find humor in Dario's comment.

"Touché," I smirked. Once the waiter was at the table, we all ordered food and drinks. Then, we ate and had idle conversation once our food was brought to our table. I may not have wanted to be friends with the twins, but I was glad we could be cordial with each other. The unexpected happened tonight, and I welcomed it with open arms. This new thing I had with Aurora was exciting, and I was glad to be doing business with the twins again. I bet Jarrah was somewhere hoping things went well between us, and Mama Charmaine was in Heaven having a laugh at us for how things turned out. Even she couldn't have called this. It was amazing to me how one woman could start and stop wars without even giving any commands. Jarrah Harper was ethereal indeed, and I was glad to be in her web of love.

Chapter 10: Back to Life

February 24, 2017
The Carter Hotel
Atlanta, Georgia

As I sat at my desk, I thought of all the things that went down in the past week. After finally calling a truce with Dario and Dustin, I had gotten my relationship back on track with Jarrah, I paid off all my debt, I started a new thing with Aurora, and I was able to get Donald out of my hair by giving him half of a million dollars, and the info he needed to contact Deandra to help him with the revenge for his sister. Deandra also informed me that she let Marcus go, so I was happy about that. I knew I needed to mend things with him, but I had so much shit to deal with inside myself before I could work on our relationship like Jarrah suggested. It had been a few days since Jarrah and the twins left for Chicago, and I already missed her presence in Atlanta. Thankfully, I wasn't completely lonely since Aurora and I had been communicating through the phone. I hadn't seen her since that day at the bar, but we made plans to get together tonight. I had been anxious all day at the thought of making love to her this time. I was horny as hell. I tried to immerse myself in work to distract myself, but that was to no avail. I picked up my cell phone and scrolled through my thread with Aurora to look at the nudes and videos she had been sending me since the night at the bar. She was so sexy with her slim body and long wavy dark hair. It was safe to say I was infatuated already. I needed to slow my role though because she was still very married.

Although I used to be a habitual cheater, I loved hard when I found a woman I actually liked for real. I loved Jarrah with everything in me, but I was a slave to my pride and ego, constantly needing to have it stroked. I went through so many women whose names I couldn't even remember. It was like I had been addicted to them. However, no matter how many I fucked, I never felt fulfilled. Jarrah was the only woman who fed my mind, body, heart, and soul. That's why it was so hard for me to let her go at first. A woman like her was rare, but I was hoping Aurora could be that for me. She could never replace Jarrah, but I needed her to fill the empty space inside me since I no longer had access to the only woman I loved. I knew it was a dream, but I wanted her to leave her husband for me. This thing with her was more than sex to me, and I hoped it was the same for her. As I stared at her pictures, I fantasized about having a life with her. It may have been farfetched, but I was planning to do all I could to make it happen. I scrolled down to a video of Aurora playing with herself with a vibrator. I stared at it and pictured myself wedged between her thighs as she stimulated her clit with the vibrator. My dick was so stiff with sexual frustration I couldn't ignore it.

I pulled my drawer open and retrieved the lotion I kept in there for moisturizing my skin. I was horny as hell, so I had to rub one out. I undid my pants as I kept my eyes on my phone. Aurora's moans on the video sent chills throughout my body. I grabbed my rigid dick after pumping some lotion in my hand and began stroking it. I threw my head back and submerged myself in the pleasure. I sped up my pace because I was feigning for an orgasm. My chest heaved as I neared climax. I picked up my phone, and began recording, so I could send Aurora a video of myself. As I came, I held the camera close to my dick, so I could get a cum shot. "Look what you made me do," I seductively said as I showed her my ejaculation. Then, I pressed send. Aurora began typing a message immediately after watching my video, and I had to admit it boosted my confidence a bit. I cleaned myself up as I waited for her to respond.
I'm jealous I wasn't there to drink you.
Don't worry. I got a lot more where that came from.
Oooo. I can't wait to taste you. I smiled hard at my phone. I felt like I was in college again.
Me either. I've been thinking about you all day.
Glad I was on your mind. Keep that energy for later tonight. I'm looking forward to it.
Good, because I am too.
See you later then. I'm in a meeting with a client. I stared at the picture Aurora sent me with her last message. It was a picture of her sitting behind her desk. She was

wearing a navy-blue blazer on top of a cream-colored bodycon cable knit dress. She was so stunning. I had to make her mine.

"Mr. Carter, there's a call for you on line one," my new assistant Janet told me through the intercom I had placed in my office, so she wouldn't have to walk back and forth. She startled me, but I wasn't mad about it. I needed a distraction before I spent the entire day in my office jacking my dick like a teenaged boy. I picked up the phone in my office and pressed line one.

"Hello, this is Mr. Carter. Who am I speaking with today?"

"Quincy? Is this really you," I heard a familiar voice say through the phone.

"Yeah Ma. This is really me," I sighed. Monalisa was quiet for a few seconds. She was processing the latest information since she thought I was dead. I took Jarrah's advice and went by my childhood home to see her over the weekend, but there was another family living there. I was shocked that she wasn't there anymore, and I was instantly worried about her. I left my hotel number with the family in case she went by there at any point. I wasn't expecting to get a phone call from her this soon though.

"I thought you were dead, Q. I thought I lost you forever," she cried. I rolled my eyes because she was being dramatic.

"I'm still here, Ma, and I ain't planning to leave no time soon," I assured her. I could hear her sniffle.

"How you been? You aight?"

Monalisa was silent for a while, then she said, "Honestly, I haven't been doing well, son. I had to sell the old house. I've been staying in a motel for the past few weeks," she told me. I felt bad for her even though I didn't want to. I took care of her for as long as I could remember, so she couldn't keep up her lifestyle without me.

"What did you do with the money you got for the house," I questioned as I furrowed my brows at her.

"I didn't get much since the house was in bad condition. I'm down to a few dollars," she admitted. I shook my head. If I had known my mother like I thought I did, I would have been willing to bet she gambled her money away. Because of my past, I couldn't judge her too much, but it did bother me that she had blown through her money. I racked my brain as I tried to think of a solution. Although I didn't care for my mother much, I wasn't okay with her being on the streets. Anything could happen to her, and I wouldn't be able to live with myself if it did.

"Ma, you can come stay with me until I can afford to get you another house," I told her. I was hesitant to invite her to my space, especially since I just started dating again, but I didn't feel comfortable leaving her out alone. Besides, this was a part of my process of becoming a better man. I knew Jarrah would be proud of me for making that step.

"Are you sure, Quincy? I don't want to impose on you," she lied. I rolled my eyes because I knew that's why she was calling me in the first place.

"Yeah, but on three conditions. No drugs, no alcohol, and no gambling. I'm not tolerating your bad habits this time around," I warned her. I could hear her exhale deeply like she was annoyed with what I said.

"Okay. I'm clean now, so you don't have to worry about that anymore," she promised me. I nodded my head.

"Where are you? I'll come pick you up on my lunch break and take you to my apartment. I have two bedrooms, so you'll have your own space," I assured her.

"I'm at the Motel 6 on South Cob Drive," she said. I shook my head. I couldn't believe she fucked her life up so much she ended up there. If she was going to stay with me, she was going to have to work on herself. My first therapy session was in a couple of days, so I'd try to lead by example. I hoped she wouldn't be resistant against it. Either way. She had to work on herself if she wanted me to take care of her.

"Aight. I'll be there in about twenty minutes."

"Q?"

"Yes ma'am?"

"I'm so happy you are alive," she acknowledged. I wasn't sure if she was saying that because I offered to help her or if she was really happy, I was alive. I hated that I couldn't trust her words to be genuine.

"Mr. Carter, there's a Kiandra here to see you," my assistant announced through the intercom, interrupting my thoughts. My blood immediately began to boil. After what she had accused me of, she had the audacity to show her face at my hotel. Half of me wanted to refuse her company, but the other half of me wanted to know why she had come.

"Ma, I have to go. I have some business to take care of," I told Monalisa.

"Okay son. See you soon," she responded. I hung up my phone and decided if I would hear Kiandra out or not.

I pressed the button on my intercom, and said, "Send her in Janet. Thank you!" After a few minutes, Kiandra entered my office and sat across from me at my desk. We stared at each other in silence for a few seconds. I was still angry at her, but I had to admit that she looked good as hell. It was my first time seeing her in civilian clothes. Under her trench coat, she was wearing a black fitted midi dress with her breasts sitting pretty, and her ass poking out. Her smooth deep brown skin shined like it was summertime, and her lips looked moisturized and luscious. I hated how weak I was when it came to her. I spent a lot of time with her in the past few years, and although we didn't have sexual intercourse until I was divorced, I was attached to her.

"Why are you here, Kiandra? Are you not satisfied with the results of you trying to ruin my life," I inquired as I tried not to stare at her breasts. She lowered her gaze and pouted, making me feel bad for coming at her aggressively.

"I just… wanted to apologize for what I did to you. I'm not proud of my actions at all. I was… in love with you, so I took it hard when you rejected me," she confessed. Her apology tugged on my heart strings a bit, but I couldn't let her get away that easily.

"What do you mean you were in love with me? You never told me that before."

"I know, but I am. I swear," she reiterated. I stared into her eyes to search for authenticity in them, and I could tell she was remorseful. I didn't know how she felt about me until she said it. I thought we wanted the same thing from each other.

"Why didn't you just say that instead of going after my career with your sexual harassment allegations," I questioned with my nostrils flared. She hung her head down and sat silently for a few seconds. Then, she stood up out of her seat, and walked over to me. My heart rate sped up as she got closer to me. I didn't want to be near her because I was weak. She got on her knees and looked up at me through puppy dog eyes. I hated that she knew that a submissive woman was my weakness.

"I am sincerely sorry, Quincy. I promise I will never do that to you again. I love you and I miss you. Please, let me make it up to you," she begged. I looked down at her and swallowed the lump in my throat. Although she was yielding to my power, she was so forward with what she wanted from me. It scared me a little. I was at a loss for words, so I sat quietly and eyed her as she pouted. After a few seconds, she started undoing my pants. I wanted to stop her, but my arms wouldn't move.

"I'm sorry baby. Please forgive me," she asked me as she stroked my dick. I exhaled deeply as I tried to keep it together. Kiandra had magical hands and her head game was astounding. That's why it was hard for me to hate her. Before she could put my dick in her mouth, I bent down to kiss her sweet lips.

"I missed you too, but you gotta prove to me that I can trust you. For now, though, show me how much you missed me," I commanded her as I held her head between my hands. I slid my hands around her neck and moved her head toward my dick. She took the whole thing in her mouth slowly as I applied pressure to her neck. I wanted her to choke on my shit as an apology. She sucked me off like my dick was the bone in the best drumstick she had ever tasted. I exhaled entirely and sunk into my seat as she deep throated me. My body felt light, and airy as she made my dick disappear.

"Mmmm," she moaned as she bobbed her head swiftly. She stroked the base of my dick with her right hand moving clockwise and her left hand moving counterclockwise.

"Shit Kiandra, you feel so good," I whispered to her. She lifted her head and opened her mouth so her spit could coat my rigid dick. I kept my eyes on her as she sucked her saliva back off of me. I loved how nasty she was. I grabbed my shaft and smacked her on her lips with it. She threw her head back and opened her mouth, so I could fuck her in her mouth. I stood up, and stirred my dick into her mouth as she sucked her cheeks in allowed me to penetrate her throat.

"Fuck, I'm about to cum," I announced before I nutted down her esophagus. She held some of my nut on her tongue to show it to me before she swallowed it. I loved the visual of my seed in her mouth. It turned me on. I brought her up to be eye level with me, so I could kiss her. She pushed her dress up and slid my dick inside her wetness. She came prepared to fuck me since she didn't have any panties on. I didn't know if I should have been upset at that or what. I pushed her against my desk and pushed her legs up. Then, I put my foot in my chair so I could dig deep inside her.

"Don't you ever betray me again," I told her as I pumped into her. We stared at each other as we tried to keep it down so my assistant wouldn't hear us.

"You hear me, Kiandra. If you want to keep getting this dick, you better not betray me again," I repeated.

"I promise I won't betray you again, Quincy. I love you so much," she moaned. I wrapped my hand around her throat and choked her as I rapidly plunged into her. She let out breathy moans, but she couldn't speak. I was restricting her breathing a little, but not enough for her to pass out. Kiandra had a fetish for being dominated, so she enjoyed every minute of what I was giving her. I was so caught in the moment; I hadn't realized I completely forgot to use a condom. I wasn't going to stop though. I would just make her swallow my seed again. After a few minutes, Kiandra coated my dick with her nectar. I pulled my dick out of her, and brought her head down, so I could nut down her throat. She sucked the cum out of my dick and cleaned off any residue with her tongue. For the first time, I squatted down and drank from her well. I used to be against giving oral to anybody besides Jarrah, but since Jarrah had moved on, it was time for me to do the same.

"Oooo," Kiandra sang as I tongued her clit and fingered her pussy like it owed me something. Within a few minutes, she was raining down on my tongue. We made eye contact while I sapped up her juices, and it was like we saw each other for the first time. I stood up and fed her potion to her off my tongue.

"You're mine and mine only. You hear me," I asked, urging her to smile.

"You don't know how long I was waiting for you to say that," she admitted to me. Then, we kissed like we had been starving for each other. What I said to her was the same bullshit I said to Aurora. I knew I was moving recklessly. Kiandra was obsessed with me, so she had a bad jealous streak. If she found out about Aurora, she would lose her shit. That's why I had to keep them as far apart as possible. Changing had been a challenging thing, especially since Jarrah wasn't here to keep me accountable. However, I was still going to work on myself. I was a single man, so a little fun wasn't going to hurt me. I could be the man Mama Charmaine and Jarrah wanted me to be and enjoy myself at the same time. I mean, what was the point of having cake if you couldn't eat it?

Chapter 11: Second Chances

February 24, 2017
Highland Square Apartment Complex
Atlanta, Georgia

Kiandra coming by the hotel unannounced distracted me a bit, so I was late getting to Monalisa. I knew she'd be there waiting for me since she didn't have another place to go. I dipped in and out of traffic, trying to get to Motel 6 as fast as I could. Atlanta traffic was crazy, so I tried to take as many back streets as I could. I had been over an hour late, so I knew my mother was thinking I wasn't going to show up. Although I went through that with her as a kid, I didn't take pride in taking her through the same thing. The way I used to feel when she abandoned me was something I wouldn't wish on my worst enemies. She was somewhere thinking I was paying her back for all the times she forgot me at the park. Until I moved in with Mama Charmaine and Jarrah, I spent most of my early childhood, either my family's house or at the park alone. She'd even forgotten me at the store a few times, and I ended up having to find my own way home. It was so bad I got used to it. Whenever it happened, I would just keep myself busy until either she found me, or I walked back home after getting tired of waiting for her. My childhood with that woman was tough to say the least. It's a miracle I even survived.

As I pulled up to Motel 6, I looked around to see if I saw Monalisa waiting outside for me. I didn't see her in the front, so I drove around the back to make sure she wasn't outside before I went inside and searched for her. When I got around back, I slowly scanned the area until my eyes spotted her sitting up against the hotel, near the dumpster. I frowned as I took in the image that was being painted to me. It looked like she was living outside the hotel instead of inside. Witnessing her looking like a homeless person broke my heart, but I tried not to jump to conclusions. I parked my SUV in front of her, and immediately got out, so she'd know it was me. When she laid eyes on me, she flashed me a smile that I had never seen from her before. I could tell she was happy to see me, and I had to admit that it caught me off guard. I told Jarrah I hated my mother, and I meant every word of it, but I was still happy to see her. It looked like she was going through tough times, which made me regret making her think I was dead. I approached Monalisa and helped her off the ground. When she was facing me, she eyed my scar, and lightly traced it with her fingers.

"Oh Q, you don't know how happy I am that you're alive," she told me. I pulled her into my arms and hugged her tight.

"I'm glad I am too, Ma," I said before pulling away from her.

"Let me help you with your things," I told her as I picked her things up off the ground and put them in the trunk of my truck. That's when the truth hit me like a sack of bricks. My mother lied to me when she said she was staying at the motel. She was staying here, but not inside. She had been sleeping on the streets for God knows how long, and that shit made me feel awful. After I packed all of her things in my SUV, I escorted her to my passenger seat, and buckled her in.

When I was in my driver's seat, I looked at her, and said, "You hungry? You wanna eat lunch with me?"

She looked at me and shook her head. I figured she was hungry since she was camped out by the dumpster. "Any place special you wanna go," I questioned. She stared out the window for a few seconds. I thought she was thinking about where she wanted to eat, but I glanced at her and saw the tears coming down her cheeks. I didn't know what she went through when she came back to Atlanta, but I knew it was all my fault. I thought I was taking a stance from her by cutting her off, but all I did was give her a taste of what my childhood was like. Although I knew she was at fault for how she raised me, I never wanted to put her through that pain.

"It's okay, Ma. You're okay now," I assured her. Then, I drove her to Atlanta Breakfast Club, and we sat down and ate lunch together. When I came back to Atlanta, I had a different picture of how things would go. My plan was to take Jarrah back from the twins and get back to my life with her. I hadn't expected to meet two women I liked and patch things up with my mother, but I was glad things turned out this way. I knew Monalisa and I had a long way to go, but this was a start, and I was going to do my part to rebuild our relationship. I just hoped she would carry her weight as well. After lunch, I took Monalisa to my apartment, and brought her things inside while she got comfortable in my second bedroom. When I was done, I stood at her bedroom door, and stared at her for a while. On many occasions, I had felt like the parent in our dynamic, but this time I felt like a kid helping out my mother.

"Your bathroom is stocked with towels, wash cloths, and all the other stuff you need, but if you need something specific just let me know and I'll get it for you. I have somewhere to go, so I'll be back soon. I'll bring you some dinner back, so you won't have to cook," I informed her. She sat on the edge of the bed and stared into space. I wanted to know what was going through her mind, but I knew it would take some time for her to open up to me. I slowly walked over to her and sat down beside her. I wrapped my arm around her waist, and she laid her head on my shoulder. I could tell she had been through a lot just by her actions.

"I don't know what you've been through in the past year, but I promise you I won't ever abandon you again. I know we don't have the best relationship, but I would like us to work on that. You're the only family I got left, Ma. I don't want to lose you too," I confessed as I thought of my last moments with Mama Charmaine before I declared war on the twins. Before I even went to Chicago, she warned me not to interfere with Jarrah's life or she'd never forgive me, and I didn't take heed to her words. I hated she had to die before I got to tell her I forgave her for what she did to me. Monalisa pulled away from me and looked into my tear-filled eyes. I had gotten emotional because I blamed myself for her suffering. I shouldn't have cut her off like I did. I thought I was standing up for myself, but all I was doing was being an asshole to her because of our history.

"Quincy, I'm so sorry for the way I've treated you throughout your life. I know I'm a terrible mother to you… and your brother. You two deserved better than your father and me. Thank you for helping me when I 've done nothing but hurt you. I don't deserve you as my son," she stated. I looked into her sad eyes, and wished our stories were different.

"Jarrah told me what happened between you two. I know you don't like her, but I want you to make amends with her. Regardless of the state of our relationship, she will always be in my life. So, I need you to accept that," I told her. She dropped her head and stared at the vinyl tile floors in her bedroom.

"I was awful to Jarrah. She lost her mother, and I treated her like trash. I don't think I deserve her forgiveness… or yours," she responded. I could tell she was remorseful of her actions towards Jarrah and me. That let me know there was room for change. I just had to motivate her to do it intentionally.

"Then, become someone who is deserving of our forgiveness. None of us are truly innocent in the way we've been going about things, but at least we can make changes and be better for ourselves, and each other."

"You're right, son. I promise, I will try to be a better person. You're giving me a place to stay and a second chance to be in your life. The least I can do is be better for you. I know I'm not perfect or have much faith in myself, but I'm willing to fix things with you."

"Good. I'll be starting therapy in a few days. We can do a session together at some point. If you want to go by yourself, I'll pay for it," I offered. She looked at me and smiled as bright as the stars in the galaxy. I loved seeing her smile. Most of my life she wore a frown, and tears like they were tattoo on her face, so seeing her smile was refreshing.

"You've grown into such a good man. Charmaine did a wonderful job raising you when I couldn't. I know it's too late, but she deserves some appreciation from me. She saved your life… more than once," she acknowledged. Her words made me shiver. I thought Mama had been wishing I would beat death when Dario shot me. So, hearing Monalisa say the same thing was amazing to me.

"Well, you can thank her by fixing things with Jarrah and me. She trained us for life's marathon, so it would be nice if you assisted us in our race."

"I promise you, son. I will do all I can to make things right. Marcus made me realize it was possible for me to be better. It scared me at first because it was too much pressure on me, but I realized I needed to face my fears for my boys. I just wish I ended things with him in a better way. Hopefully, I'll get a chance to fix things with him too," she said. I immediately felt guilty because I betrayed Marcus, so I wasn't sure if he'd ever be open to having a relationship with the two of us again. Shit, I didn't even know how he was doing since he was released from Deandra's warehouse. However, I knew I had to be honest with her about it.

"About Marcus… I'm sorry to have to tell you this, but… Marcus got caught up in the drama I started with the twins. He's not dead, but… I left him stranded with Deandra, so I don't know if he'd want to let bygones be bygones after what I did. She released him, but I failed to check on him after that. I'm so sorry, Ma. I should've protected him, but I chose revenge over my own flesh and blood," I admitted. She looked at me through eyes that held pain. The tears poured down my eyes and hers. She scooted over to me and wrapped her arms around my upper body. I nestled my face into her chest and released all of my sorrows. What I allowed to happen to Marcus ate me up every day. Although I didn't know him, I regretted leaving him as Deandra's hostage. I should have at least checked on him, but I didn't make him a priority in my life.

"It's okay, Quincy. It's okay. We'll sort this out as a family," my mother assured me as she soothed my pain. I caused a lot of people a lot of pain during my rampage. Some of them were innocent like Jarrah, Theresa and her boyfriend, and my brother, so they didn't deserve the pain and suffering I put them through. I had a lot of sins to repent for. I just hoped God would forgive me for all I had done. I definitely needed to change. I couldn't afford to cause more trouble for anyone else.

After our moment, I got myself together, and got ready to meet Aurora at my hotel. She told me she told her husband we had a business meeting, so it made sense for us to just get a room there. I had my event planner to get a suite ready for us. I wanted to wine and dine her. What we did in the bathroom was fun, but I wanted to share a romantic moment with her. I was serious about locking in with her, and I was going to see if she felt the same way about me. Sex was cool and exciting, but I was craving for some intimacy with someone I liked. Kiandra was ready for what I wanted, but I couldn't trust her, so I needed to keep her at arm's length. Aurora was the perfect woman for me on paper. She was intelligent, beautiful, ambitious, business oriented, and she was freaky as hell in the bedroom. She was the epitome of lady in the streets, freak in the sheets, and that's what turned me on the most about her. Regardless of her marital status, I was determined to make her mine.

Chapter 12: A Night of Romance

February 24, 2017
The Carter Hotel
Atlanta, Georgia

When I pulled up to The Carter Hotel, I was excited about getting to see Aurora again. This time I would have more time with her to show her how I really feel about her. I was anxious about tonight because she could reject my gesture if she weren't down for what I was down for. Her sex was amazing, and I couldn't wait until I got a chance to experience her again, but I was craving intimacy more than anything. I missed the intimate moments I used to have with Jarrah, when I could pour my heart out to her, and she wouldn't judge me. There was nothing like a woman who accepted all of you. Jarrah had been my one, but I fucked it up, so I wanted to have that with someone else. When I got to the suite, I unlocked the door, and marveled at the work my event planner had done. There was a bouquet of red roses in a vase on the dining table that was surrounded by candles, rose petals were on the floor and on the canopy bed, candles were lit around the room, and a few red and white balloons were placed in the corners of the room. The new ceiling mirrors I had installed a few months ago reflected the bed nicely, and I couldn't wait to put it to use. After I was done soaking in my event planner's handiwork, I pulled my cell phone out of my pocket, and looked at the time. It was five thirty on the dot. Aurora was supposed to meet me here at six, so I had some time to kill.

After having that conversation with my mother, my emotions had surfaced, so I hoped I could be open with Aurora about them. I didn't just see her as a cum bucket, I wanted more from her because I could tell she was the type of woman I wanted to settle down with. I knew I sounded crazy for thinking like that since she was a married woman, but when I made my mind up about something, I followed through with it. I knew there was a chance that I would get rejected, but I had to put myself out there before I allowed that to deter me. After sitting on the small velvet maroon modular sofa in the living room area of the suite for a while, I began to get restless. I looked at the time on my phone again, and it had only been five minutes since I checked it the first time. I had a while before Aurora arrived, so I needed to figure out how to kill some time. I didn't want to text her yet because I didn't want to seem too pressed, so I decided to text the people who I knew my thoughts and feelings were safe with. I opened up my messaging app and created a group with Jarrah, Theresa, and I.

Me: *Hey. Are y'all busy?*

Terry: *Wait, what? I'm included in the convo.* I chuckled as I read Theresa's message.

Jarrah: *I'm free. How are you doing Q?*

Me: *I'm doing okay. Just needed to talk to y'all really quick.*
Terry: *Mama would be so proud if she saw you right now, Q.* I shook my head at Theresa's comment before I got ready to respond.
Me: *I told you I was trying to change.*
Terry: *Yeah, you did say that.*
Jarrah: *Lol Terry leave him alone.* I smiled as I read Jarrah's message. It was cute that she was defending me.
Terry: *You right girl. What's up Q?*
Me: *I figured y'all would want to know I made the first step on fixing things with Mona.*
Jarrah: *Really? That's so good Quincy.*
Terry: *That's what's up. You're better than me. Ivanna and Ezequiel can kiss my ass.*
Me: *Smh. You would say some shit like that, Terry. Lmao*
Jarrah: *Don't mind her Q. She's salty because she can't do the same.*
Terry: *Jarrah if you hate me just say that. You ain't had to go there.*
Me: *Lmao. Y'all are hilarious. Can't lie. This brings back memories.*
Jarrah: *Sorry Terry. You walked into that one.*
Jarrah: *Is that all you wanted to tell us Quincy?* Of course, Jarrah would see through me before I got to say what I really wanted to talk to them about.
Me: *Well, Monalisa is living with me now. I'll give dets later. But what I wanted to talk about was this woman I'm interested in.*
Terry: *WHAT? A WOMAN WHO ISN'T JARRAH?*

Jarrah: *OMG Q. That's so good. I'm so proud of you. Who is she?* I couldn't help but be happy she was happy for me. However, it just clicked to me that Aurora was our accountant when we were married, so Jarrah knew her. That meant she knew she was married. I wasn't sure if I wanted to be completely honest, but a part of me wanted them to know the real.
Me: *No judgement?*
Jarrah: *Of course not.*
Terry: *I'm not making any promises.* I sucked my teeth at Theresa, but I didn't care if she judged me or not. I was used to that with her anyway. It was cool, though because I judged her too.
Me: *Her name is Aurora.*
Jarrah: *Our accountant?*
Terry: *Oooo, not the accountant.*
Me: *Yes.* I stared at the three dots by both of their names on my phone and waited anxiously for them to respond.
Jarrah: *I like Aurora, but isn't she married? Also, didn't you just have an incident with your assistant?*
Me: *Yeah, she is married. I know how it looks, but this is the first woman I've liked since you. Trust me, I know the risks. I won't get caught up.*
Jarrah: *Okay. Well, good luck with that.* I had to admit I was shocked that Jarrah responded the way she did. I expected her to tear into me a bit more. I guess she was working on letting go too.
Terry: *I don't even know enough to have an opinion, but if you like it, I love it.*
Me: *This is me trying to move on.*

Jarrah: *I understand. Just be careful.* I shook my head. I couldn't tell if she was disappointed or what, but her energy was very passive aggressive.
Me: *I'll get back with y'all later. I have something I need to do.*
Jarrah: *Okay. TTYL*
Terry: *Later Q! Make sure you wear a condom, so you won't get that man wife pregnant.* I chuckled at Theresa's comment, and exited my messenger app. I checked the time again, and it was six 'o' clock. I stood up and walked into the bathroom, so I could take a piss.

As I washed my hands, I stared at my reflection in the mirror. I knew Jarrah was right to be worried about my dealings with Aurora since she was married, but I had to try this. I may have come off as stubborn, but that's just who I was. If there were consequences I had to face, then I was willing to face them. I felt like Aurora was worth it. Like clockwork, I heard a knock on the room door, so I rushed to open it. It was safe to say I was excited to get some alone time with her. The quickie I gave her in the bathroom at the bar was exhilarating, but I was craving for something more soul serving. I opened the door to my suite and was in awe of Aurora's beauty. She was so classy, and it was so sexy to me. She had on a tan colored Gucci trench coat and some red bottom heels. I immediately got excited because I knew what was under the trench coat. I stepped aside and let her in the room, so she could see what I was on. Her eyes lit up as she scanned my romantic surprise. I closed the door and locked it. Then, I stood behind her, and wrapped my arms around her waist. I kissed her ear and rested my mouth by her earlobe as I waited for her to process everything.

"Oh my god! This is so beautiful, Quincy. Thank you for doing this for me," she exclaimed. I smiled at my success.

"I'm glad you like it. I just wanted to set a different tone for you," I told her. She broke free of my arms and turned to face me. She threw her arms around my neck and kissed my lips. I slid my hands down her posterior, and squeezed her ass when it was in my grasp. She pulled away from me, stepped six feet back and untied her trench coat, and allowed it to fall to the floor. My eyes widened as I drank her in. She was so God damned fine with her naturally slim figure. She was wearing a black sheer leopard print chemise with a garter belt and black sheer leopard stockings. Her long jet-black hair was loosely curled, and it still hung to the middle of her back. With her six-inch heels on, she was eye level with me. I was five feet and ten inches, which was above average height for men, so I wasn't complaining. I licked my lips as I scanned her body. She didn't have Jarrah or Kiandra's body, but she wore her body type well. I liked women in all shapes and sizes, so it didn't matter to me if she had a fat ass like Jarrah, or a slim, curvy body like Kiandra. I thought she was just as beautiful as they were.

"You don't know how long I've been waiting to get my hands on you again," she told me. I had to fight my urge to blush after a compliment like that.

I smiled at her, and said, "I was just thinking the same thing."

We stared at each other for a while. She had hungry eyes as she scanned my body. I was salivating at the mouth, but I tried to keep my cool. "You want a glass of wine," I asked her.

"Sure. I'd like a glass of red wine if you have it." I nodded my head at her before I walked into the dining room and got the ice bucket with the bottle of wine in it. Then, I grabbed the wine glasses, and walked over to the refrigerator, and grabbed the charcuterie board I had my chef make for me. It had strawberries, cherries, pineapples, grapes, dark chocolate fondue, marshmallows, milk chocolate pieces, whipped cream, and honey. I arranged everything on a bed tray and carried it back into the room. Aurora made herself comfortable on the bed, so I joined her. I sat the tray in between us, and poured both of us a glass of wine, and handed hers to her.

"Thank you, Mr. Carter," she gleamed. I bowed my head. She locked eyes with me for several seconds.

"You know, we should do a toast."

"To what?"

"Um… to new beginnings, loads of fun, memorable experiences, and… love," she announced. We clank our glasses before drinking our wine. I kept my eyes on her the whole time and thought of the things she named in her toast. Of course, my mind replayed love like it was on a broken vinyl. That was what my heart was set on, and I hoped she felt the same way since she proposed the toast.

"So… Mrs. Torres, how was your day," I asked her. I wanted to take this time to see if she'd let me in.

"My day was very productive, and tiresome, but thanks for asking Mr. Carter," she retorted before taking her wine to the head. She must have had one hell of a day for her to do that.

When she was done, she asked me, "How was your day?"

"My day was pretty eventful. Some unexpected things happened," I responded.

"Care to share?"

"Well… my estranged mother contacted me today. I hadn't spoken to her in about a year before today. We have a complex relationship, so I kept my distance from her in my adult life. However, I was still taking care of her, but when Jarrah and I divorced, I cut her off out of anger… Anyway, recently she had been going through some rough times, so I offered to let her live with me until I could help her get back on her feet. So, she's living with me now."

"I see. I can't imagine being away from my mother in that way. I'm glad you two are working things out, though. It takes some maturity to put your pride to the side to help someone who's hurt you," she complimented me. It sounded like she was also talking to herself while she spoke to me.

"Yeah. I'm trying to be a better man. A lot has happened in my life recently that showed me how much I was fuckin' up," I admitted. She surveyed my scar as she listened to me.

"What's the story behind that scar of yours," she inquired. I hesitated to decide if I would go there with her.

"That's a story for another day since we don't have much time together. I'd rather spend this time getting to know you better," I deflected as I adjusted myself on the bed. Her attractive smile acted as a mirror for me, so I couldn't help but smile back.

"In that case, what do you have in store for us tonight," she asked me as her erotic chestnut eyes shined at me. I stared at her for a few seconds as I thought about the things I wanted to do and say to her. I was nervous because I knew my efforts could be declined if she wasn't interested in pursuing me seriously, and I wasn't ready for that. Things had just began with us, and I wanted to hold onto her a little while longer.

Chapter 13: What's His Is Mine

February 24, 2017
The Carter Hotel
Atlanta, Georgia

Aurora's eyes were like a crystal ball that exposed my deepest desires to me. Whenever I was face to face with her, my mind was clear, and my heart disarmed the way it did when I was with Jarrah. I knew Jarrah was one of a kind, and no woman would ever come close to her, but I saw some of the same qualities Jarrah possessed in Aurora. That was why I was obsessed with her. I saw her as Jarrah's replacement. I mean, although no one could ever take her place in my life, Aurora was close enough. I needed something to focus on so I could let Jarrah live her life without me like she deserved to do, and maybe I was biting off more than I could chew, but there was only one way I was going to find out. As I sat in front of Aurora, I thought about how I would handle this night with her. I knew I had to make the best of it because she was a married woman, so I wouldn't get to be with her whenever I wanted to. If I wanted her to see me in a different light, I had to give her the best of me every chance I got to.

I poured Aurora and I another glass of wine after I decided how I was going to move. She took a sip of hers as her penetrating gaze probed me. I could tell she was trying to figure me out. I sipped my wine as well. Then, I put both of our glasses on the bed tray, grabbed a strawberry, dipped it in the warm chocolate fondue, and fed it to her. She gobbled it down and licked the chocolate residue off my fingers. I loved that she wasn't afraid to immerse herself in this experience with me. That let me know she was comfortable with me. She picked up a marshmallow, dipped it into the chocolate fondue, and fed it to me. We went back and forth like that for about three minutes. Then, I laid her back on the bed gently, picked up her wine glass, and poured a little on the exposed skin on her stomach and in her belly button. After that, I licked it all up, and slurped it from her belly button. I kissed her from her navel up to her small breast, where I kissed, licked, and sucked on them. I could fit them in my mouth, so I went in on them as she moaned and squirmed. After I was done giving her breasts some tender love and care, I kissed her up to her collarbones, and planted kisses all over them. When I got to her neck, I stuck my finger in the chocolate fondue, and spread it on her neck so I could lick it off.

"Quincy… please stop teasing me," Aurora whined as I flicked my tongue across her neck. When I was done, I kissed her smile lines, her cheek, and then I lightly brushed my lips toward her ear.

When I got there, I whispered, "I want to take my time with you. I want to make you feel better than you ever have." Then, I kissed, licked, and nibbled on her earlobe as she rubbed the back of my head.

After I was done exploring her erogenous zones on the upper half of her body, I kissed her lips. She tongued me down like she was desperate for me, which let me know I had her where I wanted her. I reluctantly unlocked my lips from hers and made a beeline to her pussy. I kissed from her pelvic bone to her pussy lips, and intentionally allowed her to feel the heat from my breath. Then, I kissed her inner thighs, calves, and her feet. After that, I pulled her heels off, so I could suck on her pretty ass toes through the stocking she was wearing. She had her toes painted white like most women liked to get when they got pedicures. I loved feet, so I was happy hers were pretty. I didn't have a foot fetish, but I appreciated every part of a woman's body, and I gave it attention while I made love to them. I may not have had the best history when it came to how I treated women in general, but when I liked or loved a woman, I naturally wanted to cater to her.

When my mouth had touched most of Aurora's body, I moved up to her pussy, and gently pulled the black G-string thong off her. I stared at her beautiful deep lustrous yellow colored vulva and almost drooled on her. Although she was skinny, her pussy was fat just like I liked it. Most of her pussy was bare, but she had a strip of straight dark hair down the middle of her vulva that was trimmed up neatly. I kissed her along her labia majora, then I gently pulled them apart, exposing a soft pink flower. Aurora's pussy had prominent inner lips, and her clitoris peeked out a little. I pushed her knees toward her, so I could watch her flower bloom. I held her thighs in my hands as I lay on my stomach, preparing to dig into her sweetness. I bowed my head like I was asking her womanhood to bless me. I slid my tongue down the left side of her labia minora until it led me to her slit. I licked around it and slid my tongue up the right side of her labia minora. I repeated that until I heard her humming praises to me.

"Quincy please. I can't take it anymore. I want more," she begged. I smirked at her pussy before I licked from her slit to her clit. Then, I licked from her clit to her slit to further tease her. I did that until she became restless.

"You ready for me feed on you," I asked her with my face still in her pussy like I was addressing it directly.

"Yes," she exclaimed. I pulled her toward me and tongued her clit. Then, I pushed my middle and pointer finger inside her.

"Aaaah," Aurora sang as I stimulated her clit and G-spot. I was putting my heart into every action I took because I wanted to communicate my intentions to her. This wasn't just sex to me. I wanted to show her I wanted her heart too. I was getting too old for meaningless sex. I needed to be more intentional. After about five minutes of me etching my signature into her walls, and marking my territory, her body jerked, and her rain fell down on me. I immediately moved to her slit and sucked her nectar out of her. She tasted so good to me I stuck my tongue inside her. I worked it like I had done with my fingers.

"Mmmm hmmm," she hummed in a loud tone, letting me know she liked what I was doing, so I went harder while I thumbed her clit.

"Oooo, yes. Right there," she cheered. I worked overtime to keep the rhythm I was using. I was on a mission to make my mark on her. I wanted her to be hooked on my sex. I knew her husband wasn't capable of putting it down like I had been doing. I was determined to get him out of the way, so I could claim what was mine.

"Mmmm. Yes Quincy. I'm almost there," she demanded, so I gave her what she wanted.

"Mmhmm. Mmhmm, I'm cumin'," she sung in a high-pitched tone. I loved the sound of pleasure from the lips of the woman whose body I was trying to conquer. Once I was done indulging in Aurora's sweet nectar, I fed her potion to her off my tongue.

She licked and sucked on my tongue like she was trying to identify the ingredients that made her shit so sweet.

"You taste so good on my tongue," I whispered into her mouth. Aurora paused for a moment. Then, she hurriedly unbuttoned my shirt. She pushed it off my arms and threw it on the floor. After that, she undid my pants, and freed my stiff dick from my boxer briefs. Without a second thought, Aurora pushed my raw dick into her pussy. She hugged my manhood so tightly I couldn't even function enough to worry about a condom. I slid into her deep as we exhaled in unison. Aurora stared fixedly at me as I stroked her slowly. I stirred my dick in her, making her part her mouth. I stuck my thumb in her mouth, and she sucked it like it was my dick. I put the balls of her feet on my shoulder, placed another pillow under her head, and positioned myself like I was about to do pushups, so I could penetrate her deeper. I bent my knees slightly, so I could thrust into the curves of her vaginal canal. My dick had a slight upward curve, so I felt like I was fitting the missing piece into her unfinished puzzle with every thrust of my hips.

"Oh my God, Quincy. You fuckin' me so good," Aurora praised as she chewed on her thin pink bottom lip. I could tell she was feeling me deep in her cervix. I may not have had the biggest dick, but I knew how to use it. Although Jarrah was more inexperienced than I was, she taught me some things that helped me to improve in the bedroom because I wasn't always as sexually adept as I am now. When I was in my early twenties, all I cared about was getting one off in any hole that was accessible to me. However, I was a grown man now, so I fucked with intention. I wanted Aurora to feel safe with me, so I took my time with her.

"I love being inside you, Aurora. You make me feel at peace when I'm with you, and I want you to be mine," I confessed. Wrinkles formed in Aurora's skull as she took in what I told her. Suddenly, tears welled up in her eyes, and I felt bad for making her sad. I slowly brushed her tears away.

"Don't cry. I would much rather you sing for me," I told her as I shifted into second gear. I got on my knees, and pushed her feet across her shoulders, and she held them in place as I pumped into her. I leaned forward and kissed her lips as our bodies collided.

"I want you, Aurora. I want you to be mine. Do you want me like I want you," I asked her. Her brows knitted in a frown as the tears continued to fall.

"I do, but-"

"No. No buts. I can tell you aren't happy in your marriage. I can see it in your face. Please let me make you happy. Let me love you," I begged her as I deep stroked her. I knew it was unfair of me to tempt her in her most vulnerable state, but I couldn't help myself. She caressed my cheek with her dainty hands.

"Aaaah, Quincy. Mmmm," she whined. I grinded into her as I pressed my forehead into hers.

"You're so fuckin' beautiful, Aurora. I gotta have you."

"Quincy… I want you too… in every way," she finally admitted. I was glad I got through to her. I could tell she was guarded. She did a decent job of putting up a front like she was happy, but I could tell she wasn't. She didn't talk much about her relationship with her husband, but I could see the sadness in her eyes. She was a woman that was denied the love that was supposed to be hers, so she wandered around looking for it. I was determined to be it for her, though.

"So be mine. Let me make you feel like this every day," I asked her, but she didn't give me an answer. I didn't want to press the issue too much because I didn't want to ruin this experience with her. I focused my attention back on pleasing her body. I put my arms around her and flipped her over so she could be on top. I slid my hand down her back, and gripped her ass while she rode me like a bull rider. She threw her head back and bounced on my dick. I gazed at her beautiful face through the mirror as she threw her hands up like she was on a rollercoaster. It was like time stood still and she was riding me in slow motion. She looked so majestic as she sat on her throne and commanded my dick to feel her pleasure.

"Aw shit. You feel so good, baby," I grunted as I watched her go up and down. As I lay on my back on the canopy bed with my legs slightly parted, Aurora threw her left leg over my hip and planted it on the bed. Her right leg touched the floor with her tiptoes. She placed her hands on my thighs and thrusted her hips into me. I guided her by placing my hand on her hips. Her pussy choked my dick like she was trying to strangle it. If that were the case, I'd gladly die by her hands. After about five minutes, I could feel the orgasm coming. I gripped Aurora's thighs and plundered her cave in search of the path that would lead me to her heart.

Then, I pushed her back on the bed, looked her deep into her curious eyes as I pumped into her, and said, "I can see the pain in your eyes even when you're smiling. All I want is to make you happy. You deserve to be happy Aurora," I convinced her as I counted each tear that fell from her eyes. They were proof that I was right about her. Although she was gorgeous, and well put together, I could see the misery in her eyes. That was why she was lying under me in the first place.

"I'm not the kind of woman you should want to save," she responded, and it broke my heart. She was too much of a good catch for her to think of herself like that.

"Don't say that, Aurora. You are worth saving to me," I countered. She stared at me for a while.

"You don't know me."

"But I want to though," I retorted. She bit into her lips and surveyed my eyes like she was trying to figure out if she could trust me.

"I promise I won't hurt you if you let me in," I vowed. She closed her eyes tight to hold back her tears. I hated to see her cry.

"Make love to me Quincy. Make me feel good again," she commanded. I lowered my head to kiss her lips gently. Then, I plunged into her with a little more force than I had been using. I could hear her pussy smacking as I fucked into her like I was a broke ass nigga, and she was my sponsor.

"Just like that Quincy," she praised as she left markings on my back. I dug into her deeper and fought my urge to nut for as long as I could. Once I felt her nectar spill on my dick, I couldn't help myself.

"Aaaah," Aurora and I moaned in unison as we orgasmed. I immediately was shocked at myself for not pulling out. I was being reckless like this woman didn't have a man at home. If I didn't pull myself together soon, I was going to open Pandora's box on our heads. I was tripping hard. I was never the type of man to be irresponsible with my dick. I made sure to keep plenty of condoms when I was fucking women, but I had been moving different lately. Maybe since I knew I would never have the family I always wanted with Jarrah was making me more comfortable with being careless. Since I decided I wanted Aurora to be Mrs. Carter, a part of me wanted to get her pregnant to seal the deal. I knew I should have learned my lesson by now, but it was hard to break old habits. Before we could come off our dopamine high, I cradled Aurora's head in my hand, and stared into her eyes.

"I know you haven't given me the answer I'm looking for, but… you will be mine. I'm going to do everything I can to make that happen," I vowed to her. She peered into my eyes, and I could see a glimpse of hope. Whether she wanted to admit it or not, she wasn't happy with her husband, and after seeing him, I could see why. He had nothing on me as far as appearances. He may have had more money than I did, but I wasn't broke, so I could take care of her financially as well. Since the twins were going to build my hotel, my wealth would increase in no time, so that wasn't an obstacle we had to get through. I just needed her to take a chance on me, so I could show her what it meant to really be loved by someone that loved her unconditionally. Her gloomy eyes would haunt me until she gave me a chance. I knew she hadn't asked me to save her from her miserable life, but after the night we just had, I was going to make that my new life's mission.

Chapter 14: Under Pressure

February 26, 2017
Highland Square Apartment Complex
Atlanta, Georgia

As I sat on the edge of my bed, I stretched the night's sleep off my body. I had been exhausted from the sex I had been having with Aurora and Kiandra. Kiandra had been laying it on me heavy like she knew there was someone else in my life. I wasn't complaining though. After the night I had with Aurora, I felt good about my chances with her. Although I hadn't seen her since then, we talked on the phone every day. I was shocked she was able to talk to me so much being that she was married, but I was quite sure her husband was the type to not be home most of time. He probably was rich as hell, always taking business trips and shit. If he was the typical rich man, he had a woman or two on the side too. Aurora never shared her personal life with me, and something about that made me uneasy. I needed to know who I was up against, so I'd know how to move. That's why I asked my private investigator to find out about Aurora's husband. I needed to know the shit I would have to go through to take her from him, so I could decide if it were worth it. Aurora was my dream girl, so I thought she was worth my trouble. However, I didn't want a repeat of what I just went through with Jarrah and the twins. That was too much for me. I needed to play this cool to avoid that.

Tired of my mind wandering, I went into my bathroom, showered, and freshened up. Then, I made my way to Monalisa's room door. Ever since I brought her to stay at my apartment, she had been couped up in the house. We hadn't spoken in detail, so I didn't know how she was feeling. I was barely home because I was either working or with Kiandra or Aurora, so I barely gave her any of my attention. It had been difficult and draining to go back and forth to all three of my hotels, and I was about to have one in Chicago, so it would be more for me to juggle. Honestly, things were getting too difficult for me to handle alone. It was time for me to find someone who was interested in running my business for me. I fucked up my deal with Mr. Patel, so I needed to find someone else to manage my hotels for me. When I first decided to open up my hotel, I had gone into it with the desire to handle everything myself, but since my franchise was growing, I needed someone to manage things for me, so I wouldn't have to be hands on all of the time. I was slowly becoming the businessman I wanted to be, so I needed to relinquish some of my control. Once I got to Monalisa's room door, I knocked.

"Yes," she called out to me.

"Ma are you decent," I asked her. I wanted to make sure she had her privacy while she was here, so she wouldn't feel like my child.

"Give me a minute," she told me. I waited for her to give me permission to enter. I could hear her shuffling around inside her room. I hoped she was getting dressed, and not hiding anything from me. She had been a recluse since she got here, so I hoped she wasn't lying to me about being sober. Her behavior was looking a little too familiar to me, and I wasn't feeling it. I was glad my first day of therapy was tomorrow because I had a feeling, I'd need a shrink to help me deal with my mother. After about two minutes, Monalisa opened the door. I looked her over and peeked over her to check things out in her room.

"Is there something you wanted Q," she questioned. I looked into her eyes to see if she was high. Her eyes looked normal enough to me. I hated that it was the first thing that came to my mind, but that was usually the case with her.

"I came to see if you wanted to get out for a while. You've been in here since you came," I told her. She stared at me for a while.

"I don't know, Quincy. I've been so tired lately," she said.

"I understand, but I think getting some sun will do you some good."

Monalisa breathed out warm air as she processed what I told her. "Okay Quincy. I'll do it for you. Just give me a minute to get ready," she replied. I was glad she was willing to get out because I was worried about her. I could tell she was depressed, which scared me a little.

My mother had suicidal tendencies ever since I was a kid. I couldn't even count the number of times I found her pass out in the bathtub in her own blood because she slit her wrist. She even tried to overdose on drugs as well. Those images of her would forever be traumatic for me. I remember hating myself as a kid because I felt like I wasn't enough for my mother to want to live for. I knew what she did wasn't my fault, but it didn't stop me from thinking I was a burden on her. That's why I eventually asked Mama Charmaine to take me in. I couldn't handle the thought of Monalisa being successful in one of her suicide attempts. While I waited for Monalisa, I sat in my living room, and let my mind wander. Lately, I had been clouded with so many thoughts that it was hard to live in reality. I was always in my head, and it was getting stressful. For once, I wanted things to align for me and work out. I was tired of having to work so hard at everything to have a decent life. When I was in a relationship with Jarrah, most of my days were good. I didn't feel as much pressure when I was with her as I did after leaving her. I missed someone having my back like Jarrah did. Suddenly, I got the urge to hear her voice, so I pulled out my cellphone, and dialed her number. The phone rang three times before I got an answer.

"Hello," one of the twins said through the phone, making me frown. I checked my phone to verify that I dialed the right number, and I did. I assumed it was Dario because I didn't think Dustin was the type to pull something like that.

"What's up man? Is Jarrah around," I asked him. He paused for a while as if he were deciding if he was going to let me talk to her or not.

"Yeah, she's right here. Hold on for a minute," he told me before he handed her cell phone to her. I could tell he wasn't a fan of our arrangement, but I didn't care as long as Jarrah was.

"Hello," Jarrah said once she had the phone. My mind was instantly at ease.

"Hey, Jarrah," I responded.

"Everything okay Q," she immediately asked like she was a clairvoyant. I let out my breath like I was releasing my problems into the atmosphere.

"It's that bad," she said before I could say anything. She reminded me so much of Mama, and it was bittersweet because I missed her so much, but I was glad she left her imprint on Jarrah.

"I'm just having one of those days," I finally admitted.

"What's wrong?"

"Nothing and everything at the same time," I responded. I could hear Jarrah sigh.

"Spit it out Q," she demanded. I shook my head as I decided where to start. I looked around like I felt someone watching me. Then, I went to my bedroom, so I could talk in private. I didn't want my mother to hear me discussing her with Jarrah.

"Well, I've just been feeling like I'm under so much pressure lately. I hadn't realized it until now, but you spoiled me. I'm so used to you having my back, so I've been struggling. Juggling three hotels is bad enough, but soon I'll have a fourth one to add to the weight already on me. Then, there's my dating life, and... I'm worried about Monalisa," I elaborated. I could hear Jarrah switch her phone from one ear to the other one. While I waited, I realized I hadn't bothered to ask how she was doing. I just called her with my issues without checking if she was okay to deal with it first.

"I'm so sorry, Jarrah. I didn't check in with you before I unloaded on you. How are you?"

"I'm okay Quincy. You're fine. I'm on bed rest for a few weeks, so all I have is time. I decided to take a break from work until I give birth. So, you're doing me a favor in a way by giving me something to do," she explained. I was relieved that I hadn't offended her by what I did. However, hearing that she was on bed rest alarmed me. I hoped she didn't lose another baby because of the shit I put her through. I wouldn't be able to live with myself if she did.

"Are you okay?"

"Yeah. Things have been rough, but that's how pregnancy can be. I have been through a lot of stress, so that contributed to it, but I'll be fine. This time is going to be different. I'm going to have a healthy baby in a few months. Dario and Dustin have been making sure of that," she giggled. I smiled by reflex, but I felt like shit. I really screwed up her life this time, and I needed to figure out how to repay her for all the trouble I caused.

"I understand that I have to stop running to you every time I have a problem. I-"

"Q please! We are family, and we will always be family. I said it was okay. I'm gonna be fine. You just worry about yourself," she commanded in a stern voice. She sounded so much like Mama that it was scary.

"Okay Mama Jr.," I joked. She giggled, and I couldn't help but chuckle too.

"I miss her so much," I said as our laughter died down.

"So do I… You know Q, you are capable of getting things in order yourself. You don't need me, and you never did. Hire someone to manage the hotels for you, so you won't have to be so involved. I have a few numbers I can send to you by text if you want them."

"Thank you, Jarrah! I definitely need them."

"It's no problem at all. After you hire someone, take a vacation so you can recuperate. You've been through some traumatic events too, so you need to get back on track mentally and physically. You don't have to walk around like shit didn't happen to you too. Yeah, you did some terrible things, but you also had some terrible things done to you… and about your mother. Take care of her Quincy. Do everything you can to help her out. You need her just as much as she needs you. Don't forget that, and don't let her forget it," Jarrah instructed. I nodded my head like she was in the room with me. Everything she said was on point. I knew she was who I needed to talk to, to get my mind right.

"You're right about everything as usual," I complimented.

"Of course, I am. Don't hesitate to call me if you need me. We promised Mama we were going to continue to be a family, so we will keep that promise. Besides… I'm bored, so hearing about your drama will give me something to occupy my time," Jarrah teased. My mouth stretched across my face and curved up into a smile.

"I bet. Don't you hesitate to call me either. I don't want this to feel like a one-sided friendship to you," I told her.

"Okay. You got it!"

"Good. I'll talk to you later, Jarrah. I'm about to take Monalisa out, so she can get some fresh air."

"Okay Quincy. Make sure you two have fun," she reminded me.

"I will," I responded before we hung up. My conversations with her always gave me clarity, and I was happy for that. I left out of my bedroom and went back into my living room. My mom was sitting in there waiting for me.

I walked over to her, held my arm out for her to lock hers in mine, and asked, "You ready to go, young lady?" Monalisa flashed me a faint smile before she slowly stood up and interlocked her arm in mine. She nodded to answer me before we started out of the door. I hated seeing my mother sad, and if memory served me right, I needed to do all I could to keep her from trying to leave this life too soon.

Chapter 15: Monalisa's Smile

February 26, 2017
Historic Fourth Ward Park
Atlanta, Georgia

When we pulled up to the Historic Fourth Ward Park in Atlanta, I put my SUV in park, unbuckled my seatbelt, and walked to the passenger side of the car to escort my mother out of it. Then, I walked back around to the driver's side, and got our brunch out of the backseat. Mona and I slowly walked to the seating area of the Skate Park, and found a vacant spot to sit in. The park wasn't packed today, so there was plenty of space for us to have some alone time. There was a band set up at the bottom of the stairs playing jazz music, so it was a cool Sunday afternoon vibe. I laid down a blanket on the cement and helped Monalisa in her seat. Then, I wrapped a blanket around her. The temperature was in the low seventies all week, so it wasn't too cold or too warm outside. However, my mother was anemic, so I knew she'd need some extra layers. I sat beside her on the blanket, and got our food situated. Atlanta Breakfast Club was packed when we went, so we settled for Waffle House instead. I'm sure Monalisa didn't mind it since she loved Waffle House since I was a kid, but I hadn't eaten there in years. I ordered the All-Star Special for both of us, and we quietly dug into our food once we were settled.

As I ate, I took in the atmosphere, and couldn't help but love my city. The way people just came together in various places and celebrated life amazed me. Being in Chicago had influenced me to behave in a way uncommon for me. However, after I returned back home to Atlanta, I was reminded of who I really was. If I had known things would escalate to the level they did, I would have stayed my black ass here and let Jarrah have her new life. Who was I kidding? I would have made the same decisions all over again because I loved her so much, and I couldn't imagine my life without her. I was glad things ended the way they did even though I didn't get my wife back. Now that I had been at my lowest, I could meet my mother with compassion rather than anger and resentment like I used to. I turned my attention to Mona and looked her over for a few seconds. Instinctively, my attention turned toward her wrists, where she wore proof of her hard life. That's when I noticed a cut that looked fresh. It looked like she had begun to cut herself but stopped for some reason. That's when it clicked to me. She was shuffling around in her room because I caught her in one of her weak moments. As I stared at her wrists, she turned her attention to me, and shifted in her seat, so I wouldn't see her wrist anymore.

I stared in her face since she refused to look me in my eyes, and said, "You know, you don't have to hide things from me anymore, Ma. I'm not a little boy anymore, and… if I'm being honest, even back then I knew you were suffering. It never made me feel good that you were going through it, and I couldn't help you. I took it to heart back then, and I do now. Please don't hide things from me. Just let me help you." She held her head down, so I cupped her cheek in my hand, and turned her face toward me.

"Ma, I love you so much. I know I've been a terrible son to you throughout the years, but I love you. Please don't check out on me. I need you. You're all I got," I confessed. Tears fell from her eyes as she looked at me. I grabbed her and pulled her into my arms. I stroked her hair as she cried on my shoulder.

"It's okay, Ma. You're going to be okay. I'll make sure of that," I vowed to her. After about two minutes, she pulled away from me. I handed her a paper towel, so she could dry her eyes and clean her nose. I could tell she was crying all night because her eyes were puffy and dry.

"I'm sorry I'm making things hard for you. I don't want to feel like I'm a burden on you. You've gone out of your way to help me, so I don't want to give you a tough time," she confessed after she got ahold of her emotions. I grabbed her hand and held it, so she would know what I was about to say was sincere.

"You aren't a burden to me. I decided I wanted to help you. What kind of son would I be if I allowed you to stay on the streets? I don't want that life for you. I know life has been a struggle for you, so I want to help end your suffering if I can. Why didn't you come to one of my hotels or my apartment when you needed help," I asked her.

"I thought that you were dead, and since Jarrah's name was still on everything you owned, I figured I wouldn't have been able to go there without you being there," she explained. I didn't feel bad for keeping Jarrah as my beneficiary and giving her the rights, she had as my wife since she was the most dependable person in my life, other than Mama Charmaine. My mother proved she wasn't capable of owning anything lucrative, so it would have been stupid of me to give her rights. However, I did wish I could trust her enough to do that.

"You could have reached out to Jarrah. She would have helped you as long as you respected her," I told her.

"I was too proud to be respectful when I did reach out, but… Dustin gave me five thousand dollars to get back to Atlanta, and to take care of myself for a while," she responded. I was shocked to hear that he helped her, but I wasn't at the same time. If anybody were kind enough to help my mother, it would be him. I was glad he was kind enough to do that for her, and I gained a new level of respect for him.

"Why did you sell the house then?"

Monalisa shifted in her seat, so I knew she was about to give me some bad news. "I uh… I was behind on my payments, and what he gave me wasn't enough to cover that, and the utilities," she told me. I frowned at her.

"Behind on payments? I paid the house off, so you wouldn't have to pay rent. Did you take out a mortgage or something," I questioned. She lowered her head, giving me my answer. I shook my head. I couldn't believe she would do that after I worked so hard to pay that house off for her. I tried not to be too mad at her though since we were trying to move forward.

"How much were you behind?"

"I was approved for two hundred and fifty thousand," she admitted.

"Two hundred and fifty thousand," I repeated loudly before she could even get it all out. I couldn't believe she would take out a loan for that much when she knew she couldn't pay it back. The lenders knew that shit too. I hated the credit and loan system. That shit did nothing but keep the impoverished in poverty. It took me a while to develop a healthy relationship with that system, and I had Mama Charmaine to thank for instilling that in me because God knows the woman sitting in front of me was incapable. I took a deep breath to calm myself down since I could tell she was embarrassed by it.

"How much do you owe?"

She shrugged her shoulders, and said, "I don't remember how much I owed. I hadn't made a payment in over three months. I stopped keeping up with it because I didn't have the money to pay it. Before I went looking for you, they came and told me they were going to foreclose it. That's when I went to Chicago to find you because I needed your help paying it back. Since you were supposed to be dead, I returned home, and contacted them. They advised me to do something called a short sale, so I advertised it in the paper with some of the money that twin gave me, and in a few days, someone bought it from me. I didn't get to keep any of the money though. All of it went to the lenders. They pitied me, so they forgave the remaining balance. I took what I had left of the five thousand and went to Motel 6. I ran out of money a few days ago, so I had to check out of the room. The owner did allow me to use the shower everyday though, and they gave me leftovers from the restaurant there," she elaborated. Hearing what she had been through made me pity her, but I couldn't help but think she brought all of it on herself.

Thankfully, she crossed paths with kindhearted people because things could have been worse for her.

"So, you were lying when you told me you got money from selling the house," I asked rhetorically. She bowed her head.

"I'm glad you had people looking out for you the best way they could, but I wished you had gone to one of my hotels. Dead or alive, you have a place there. Everyone knows you're my mother, so they would have helped you… It's okay though. You're with me now. We'll get things back on track," I assured her. She nodded at me.

"I'm going to get you an appointment with a therapist in the same office I will be going to. I can tell you've been cutting recently. Some of those marks on your wrists look new. I'm glad I was able to intervene before you were able to do it again," I told her, letting her know I knew she was cutting before I went to her room door earlier.

"I'm sorry son. I just… I want my sadness to end. I'm tired. I'm so tired of fighting," she acknowledged with tears in her eyes. Hearing that made me feel bad for her. I couldn't understand how she felt because I had never experienced depression. I did see her going through it throughout my life, though, so I had sympathy for her. I stroked her wrist with my thumb as I looked into her eyes.

"We're going to fix this, and you're going to feel better soon. I promise Ma," I declared through hopeful eyes. She looked into my eyes like I was unrecognizable to her. I knew my mother wasn't used to me being this patient and understanding with her because I had been the opposite for most of my life. However, what Jarrah said to me earlier inspired me to be different with my mother this time around. I already lost one mother. I didn't want to lose another one. I gathered our scraps from our brunch and stood up to put them in the trashcan.

When I got back to where we were sitting, I reached my hand out to my mother, and said, "Come on! Let's dance." Her brows knitted in a frown as she thought over what I said.

"Quincy I-," she was about to say, but I grabbed her hand and gently tugged on her until she was standing.

"I'm not taking no for an answer," I told her after interrupting her. I guided her to the bottom of the stairs where the band was playing. Once we were down there, I wrapped my left arm around her waist, and held her left hand up with my right hand. Then, I began two stepping. Mona was hesitant at first. She kept looking around to see who was watching her like she was embarrassed to dance with me.

"Keep your eyes on me woman. I'm your dance partner right now. Don't worry about anything else. It's just you and me," I assured her. She stared into my eyes and followed my lead. We two stepped and swayed from side to side to the beat of the music. After a while, other people started to join us on the dance floor. I spun her around a few times as she flashed me that beautiful smile I wasn't used to seeing. It made me realize this should be my goal when I deal with my mother from now on. I needed to do all I could to make her smile as much as I could while I had her in my life. Jarrah was right. I needed Monalisa just as much as she needed me, and I was determined to show her that every day because nothing was more beautiful to me than when Monalisa smiled.

Chapter 16: Narcissistic Tendencies

February 27, 2017
Afrocentric Counseling Center
Atlanta, Georgia

My stomach grumbled as I sat in the waiting area of the therapist's office. I was so nervous to sit in front of a stranger and bare my soul to them. Aside from Jarrah, I didn't have many people I felt comfortable talking to about my problems. However, I made the decision to see a therapist myself, and I owed it to myself to go into this new experience with an open mind. The day I had with Monalisa yesterday was the most fun I had in a while. Although it took a while for her to warm up to me, I was finally able to get her to let her hair down for a while. After we left the park, we went back home, and had a movie night for the first time. Seeing her laugh and smile as much as she did made me feel good about the development of our relationship. It gave me hope that things would continue to get better as time went on. However, although I saw a lot of positives yesterday, I knew we still had a long way to go.

Given our past, laughs and smiles weren't enough to repair our relationship. We needed so much more than that. The life I lived with Monalisa made me resent her, and Mama Charmaine stepping in to give me what my mother couldn't, didn't make things better for my relationship with my mother. While it did make my life turn out better than it could have, it didn't make me resent my mother any less. It actually was a constant reminder that my own mother couldn't give me the love some strange woman and her daughter was immediately willing to give me. Getting love from Jarrah and Mama only made me hate Mona for not wanting me. My mother told me out of her own mouth on many occasions that the only reason I was alive was because I was the only thing she had left of my father, meaning she only kept me because she couldn't let go of a man that was no longer able to love her. I still remember how I felt when she would say things like that to me. Thinking about it put me in a bad mood, but I knew at some point, my therapist was going to dig in my past to figure out why I was the way I was, so I had to prepare myself for those tough conversations.

"Quincy Carter," the receptionist called out to me, breaking my train of thought. I turned my attention to her.

"The doctor is ready to see you now," she told me. I nodded my head at her, and I exhaled deeply before standing up and making my way back. When I got halfway down the hall, I saw a short stocky black man standing in front of the door, waiting for me.

"Are you Mr. Carter," he asked me when I was in front of him. I looked him up and down for a few seconds. To say that he was a doctor, his appearance suggested otherwise. He wasn't dress in a clean, tailor-made suit like I assumed he would be in. He had on a casual hunter green button-up long-sleeved collar shirt that looked like it came from Walmart, a black tie that went past his beltline, wrinkled gray slacks, and some off brand dress shoes that looked too big for his size. I hated to judge his appearance, but it was hard not to. It looked like he threw that outfit together in the dark. I immediately second guessed my choice in therapist. However, I needed someone to talk to other than Jarrah, and I was already here, so I was going to see how it would go.

"Yes, I'm Mr. Carter," I told him as I accepted his handshake. His hands were sweaty as hell. I was so disgusted with him, but I tried to hold it in.

"Nice to meet you, Mr. Carter. I'm Dr. Charles McFarlane. Come inside and make yourself comfortable," he instructed me. I walked past him, and sat upright on the emerald, green chaise lounge sofa he had inside his office. I didn't feel comfortable enough to put my feet up in the sofa and lay back on the pillows, so I sat in the middle of the chair. As I waited for him to take his seat, I scanned the room, and noticed a lot of awards on his walls and shelves. He may not have looked the part, but something told me he was good at his job. I was hoping my assumption was true because I didn't know if I was committed enough to switch therapists as many times as it took for me to find a good one that complemented me. Dr. McFarlane waddled over to the gold reclining chaise lounge sofa that sat directly in front of me and sat down after he pushed the footrest part of it to the left of the room.

"So, Mr. Carter, how are you doing today," he asked me as he sat with his hands in his lap. I expected him to have the notepad and pen ready to write notes about my life, but as he waited for me to respond, he pulled a small voice recorder out of his pocket, and pressed what I assumed was record on it. It made me uneasy, but I knew I needed to trust the process.

I cleared my throat and responded. "I'm doing okay. A little nervous though."

"It's totally normal for you to be a little nervous for your first session with a therapist. You can relax though. The first session is usually spent on getting to know you. I'll try to stay away from the hard stuff today," he explained to me. It did calm me a bit, but I was perfectly fine with jumping into the hard stuff right away. I had a lot of mess to sort through, so I needed all the time I could get dealing with it.

"Okay," I responded.

"With that being said… could you tell me what you do for a living?"

"Well, I work in the hospitality industry. I own three hotels in Atlanta, and I'm having one built in Chicago," I responded as I straightened my posture. He pursed his lips and nodded his head as if he were giving me his approval for my line of work.

"Oh really? That's great, Mr. Carter. Congratulations," he told me. I flashed him an eager smile. No one had ever congratulated me for owning hotels before. People usually thought it was interesting, but not anything special.

"Thank you," I exclaimed. He bowed his head.

"You're welcome. What made you want to open a hotel in Chicago?"

"Well, my father was from Chicago, so I wanted to open one in his hometown to pay homage to him," I responded.

"Okay. Is your father still alive," he inquired through beady eyes. I hesitated for a few seconds because my father's death was a touchy subject for me since there was a lot of mystery surrounding his murder.

"No, he was shot before I was born," I responded, keeping it short.

"Hmm, I see," Mr. McFarlane said as he glared daggers through me. I felt uneasy because it seemed like he could see through me.

"What about your mother? Is she still alive?"

"Yeah, she is. She actually just moved in with me a few days ago," I told him. He pursed his mouth and shook his head at me again. I figured this was a habit of his when he was processing things. I tried not to take it personal though.

"Really? Why is she living with you," he inquired. I stared at him through suspicious eyes. I was trying to figure out why he was asking me these questions after saying we wouldn't get this deep today.

"She fell on hard times recently and didn't have a place to go."

"Couldn't you have just helped her out without moving her into your space," he questioned. He had a good point. Jarrah gave me six of the twelve million dollars she won during the divorce back and after giving Donald half a million to get out of my hair, I had five point five million of that money left. Plus, I didn't have to touch it since I already had over half a million, so I had the money to buy my mother a house. That would have been the decision I made if I were still with Jarrah.

"Yeah," I responded.

"Why didn't you?"

I sat quietly and thought carefully about it. It would have been easy for me to use my finances as an excuse, but I wasn't broke. It was nothing to buy my mother a one hundred- and fifty-thousand-dollar house or better yet a condominium for a little more. "If I'm being honest, I let her live with me because I was lonely. I just got a divorce from the woman I loved more than anything, and it's been hard for me to adjust to being without her. Having my mother around filled that void Jarrah, my ex-wife, emptied when she left me. Plus, when I saw my mother in the state she was in, I was terrified I would lose her for good. I just lost two people who were important to me. One of them was never coming back, so I didn't want to think about losing someone else," I confessed, deciding to be honest. I was shocked, but proud of myself. Dr. McFarlane nodded his head as he processed everything I said.

"Tell me a little about your ex-wife," he instructed. I shifted in my seat. I was nervous to bring up Jarrah because you could tell a lot about me by how I spoke of her.

"Jarrah is… one of the best people I've met in my life. I met her when I was seven years old, and we have been inseparable ever since. Well, until I divorced her… Anyways, Jarrah is selfless, kind, patient, intelligent, and she just brought me so much peace. I knew I wanted to marry her the first time I saw her. When my mother wasn't able to love me, she did, and her mother too. They took me in when I was about thirteen years old. Monalisa was strung out on drugs and alcohol, so she would forget about me like I didn't exist. Jarrah and Mama Charmaine always came to my rescue though. I loved and appreciated them for it. I just didn't know how to show it. I did so many things to hurt Jarrah in particular, and she kept forgiving me. However, when I took things too far and divorced her, I lost her forever. If I had known I would never get her back, I wouldn't have allowed her to leave me," I acknowledged.

"Hearing that you were the one to want the divorce is shocking to me being that you loved her so much. Why did you ask for the divorce?"

"Well, from the moment I made Jarrah my wife, I knew I wanted to have a huge family with her. So, after we got married, I had been desperately trying to get her pregnant, but… it never happened for us. It made me angry. I didn't understand why I couldn't have the life I wanted with her. I was obsessed with being a father, so I punished her for taking that away from me. My ultimate punishment was divorcing her. I figured I deserved someone who could give me everything I wanted. Although Jarrah was the perfect wife, I couldn't get over that one thing."

"Did you try to reconcile things with her? If so, why?"

"After I spent a year away from her, my life just fell apart. I got myself into some debt, I got in some trouble for sleeping with one of my employees, and I wasn't doing well mentally. When Jarrah first moved to Chicago, I had a private investigator check in on her every now and then. One day, he called and told me he saw a guy following her home, and he didn't leave her condo until the next morning. Hearing that alarmed me, so I went to Chicago to get my wife back. I'll admit that a part of me assumed Jarrah would never move on because I knew how much she loved me. Plus, I was her first everything, and that was special to both of us. So, it hurt me that she replaced me so soon. The final limit was when I found out she was pregnant for the new guy. Instead of just accepting it, and leaving her alone to live her life, I caused a lot of trouble for her. I ended up connecting with some people that wanted to bring down the guys she was dating, and we worked together to make their lives hell. It ended up getting her kidnapped, and I almost lost my life. She ended up miscarrying, so I saw that as a sign for me to keep trying to get her back. So, I did. Eventually, she ended the war by deciding to give all of us what we wanted, which was to have her in our lives. I had to settle for being her friend, but to me that was better than nothing," I elaborated.

"Hmm. I see," my therapist said to me. I was immediately defensive because I felt like he was judging me. I sat quietly as I waited for him to respond. I had done a lot of talking, so I knew he knew enough to get a good understanding of who I was.

"One more question, Mr. Carter... Why did you decide to come to therapy," he questioned. I exhaled deeply and sunk into my seat a bit.

"Well, losing my wife showed me I didn't have everything figured out like I thought I did. The way I ruined her life just because she wasn't accessible to me like I wanted her to be, showed me something was seriously wrong with me. I knew I couldn't figure it out myself because I don't have the best self-awareness. Aside from the way I grew up, I thought I was perfect. I did everything I was always told I was supposed to do to access the American dream, and the minute I got it, I threw it all away when one thing didn't go my way. I just couldn't let go of that one thing and come to find out Jarrah was capable of bearing my children. However, since I was such a horrible person to her, she wasn't able to hold our kids to term. So, it was my fault we didn't have kids together, and I was so obsessed with it that she felt like she couldn't even tell me the truth when we were married. So, in short, the reason I'm here is because I need some direction. I need someone to give me the tools I need to deal with things in a healthier way," I told him.

"Okay Mr. Carter. Well, considering everything you've told me, from your childhood to this point, I can say with confidence that you are a narcissist."

"What," I questioned. I didn't understand how he came to that conclusion after I told him about my upbringing. I was simply playing the cards that were dealt to me. That didn't make me a narcissist.

"Your parents were narcissistic people as well, so you internalized it, and became a different version of them. It seems like everything has to be about you, and when it's not about you, you find a way to make it about you. For instance, you speak highly of your ex-wife. You even go as far as saying she was the perfect wife. However, the minute she showed some signs of imperfection, you rejected her because she couldn't live up to your perfect idea of her. Then, when you saw she was moving on, you did everything in your power to mess it up, trying to force her to make her life all about you again. Also, your inability to be alone, and your obsession with being a parent plays a part. Did you ever question why you wanted kids so bad?"

"No, I didn't," I answered, not knowing where he was going with that question.

"Well, it seems like you have this desire to control everything around you. Being a parent to kids that have to rely on you to survive can make you feel powerful. Your mother and father did it with you, and you were trying to do the same with your own children. It seems to me that you have an unhealthy addiction to power or being in control in every aspect of your life. As I listened to you talk about your life, I could see narcissistic traits in you like arrogance, self-centeredness, apathy for others, manipulative tendencies, selfishness, and a demanding nature. Although you came to therapy on your own volition, it wasn't because you thought you needed it. You came here because you wanted to prove to your ex-wife that you were trying to become a better man, in hopes that it would bring her back to you," he accused. I glared at him. I couldn't believe he had the audacity to accuse me of doing something so asinine. I came to him because I needed help getting my life back on track, but I refused to allow someone who was dressed like a middle school English teacher to tell me anything different.

"I was a fool to think a man like you could help me. You can't even pick out a decent outfit for yourself to wear. Obviously, I made a mistake by coming here," I said as I shook my head. Then, I stood up, and adjusted my navy-blue Cooper solid hopsack Tom

Ford suit, and started out of his office as he followed behind me.

As I opened the door, he said, "Make sure you give my receptionist a call when you're actually ready to work on yourself, Mr. Carter." I kept walking like I didn't hear him. I couldn't believe a man who was supposed to be a professional doctor called himself challenging me about my own life. He was way off by suggesting I was a narcissist. I had suffered my whole life because of my parents, so the way I turned out had a lot to do with them. Although I wasn't the best person sometimes, I wasn't self-centered. I may have caused Jarrah some trouble, but that was only because she betrayed me by getting pregnant for another man. She was supposed to be my wife, and she abandoned me by moving to Chicago. Yet, I still loved her. I even went to Chicago to fix things with her, but she moved on quickly like what we had meant nothing to her. Despite what he said, I did care about people, and had no issues not being the center of attention. I allowed my mother to live with me for Christ's sake, so how was I apathetic to people. If I were a narcissist, I would have let her ass stay in the streets, especially since she wasn't a good parent to me. However, I was compassionate enough to open my doors to her. That didn't make me a narcissist. That made me a damn good son. I decided to go to therapy, so I could improve myself, but it was obvious to me that it wasn't a good idea. So much for being a good man.

Being someone that demanded his respect was more important to me anyway.

Chapter 17: Man in the Mirror

March 3, 2017
251 North Apartments Atlanta
Atlanta, Georgia

Disgust was what I felt as I stood at Kiandra's apartment door, and waited for her to let me in. I hated coming over here to the hood to see her, but she always made it worth my while. I knocked for the fifth time, and listened closely to see if I could hear her in there. I couldn't hear anything, so I started back to my Lincoln. Thank God Kiandra lived on the first floor because I wouldn't have felt comfortable leaving my new SUV outside this ratchet ass apartment complex. Don't get me wrong. Kiandra's apartment wasn't anything to turn your nose up at if you were in her tax bracket, but my money gave me access to the finer things in life, so I had grown accustomed to having them. There was no way I could ever forget where I came from because my mother was a constant reminder, but I damn sure was going to enjoy where I was. However, I understood that Kiandra didn't have what I had. As soon as I pressed the button on my key fob to unlock my SUV, I saw her swiftly walking towards me from the direction of the gym.

Kiandra jumped into my arms when she was near me. It boosted my ego. I loved that she was crazy about me even though I didn't actually feel the same way about her. She wrapped her arms around my neck and kissed me passionately. I knew what she was on how she stuck her tongue into my mouth. Kiandra's love language was physical touch just like mine, so we were always on one accord when it came to expressing our feelings to each other. I may not have been in love with her, but I still had love for her. Unlike Aurora, she was always accessible to me, and I didn't have to go out of my way to impress her. Since she didn't have much, everything I had was a lot to her, and that made me feel like I had something to offer her, while I was sure Aurora's husband's pockets were a lot deeper than mine. So, she expected the best while Kiandra appreciated what I could do for her. Kiandra pulled away from me and peered into my eyes with her pretty mahogany brown eyes that almost looked black.

"I missed you so much, Daddy," she told me. I put her back on the ground and looked down at her.

"Oh yeah? You wanna show me how much," I asked her. Her face lit up as she smiled at me. I was happy she was in a good mood because that meant I was going to get the best of her. She grabbed my free hand and tugged me into the direction of her apartment. I locked my SUV door as I followed her. Once she unlocked her door, she pulled me into her apartment, and dropped down on her knees before she got to close the door behind us. Since she was preoccupied, I closed the door for her, and began helping her strip me. I stood in front of her butt ass naked as I waited for her to suck me off. She looked me up and down through lustful eyes and gloated.

"Damn you're fine as hell," she said before saying something else in Patois. I loved when she spoke Patois, even though I didn't understand what the fuck she was saying. She eased her pretty brown lips on my dick, sucked her cheeks in, and bobbed her head on me like it had her favorite flavor on it. I threw my head back and exhaled as pleasure consumed my body. Kiandra may not have been someone I could see myself marrying, but she was great side piece material. She was so good at sucking my dick I became addicted to her.

"Aw fuck," I groaned as Kiandra performed her signature head bob and stroke combo on me. Then, she took my dick so far down her throat she vomited. The first time she did that to me, it grossed me out, but I became obsessed with it. I ejaculated right after, and I pulled my dick out of her mouth and allowed the vomit to fall on the floor. Kiandra quicky got up and got something to clean the mess she made off my dick and the floor. She may have been nasty in the bathroom, but she kept her place clean as fuck. It was like she had OCD. While she rinsed her mouth and put the rag back, I sat on her couch and stroked my dick as I waited for her to return. I wanted to warm myself up, so she wouldn't have to. After about two minutes, she came back to the living room dressed in a nurse costume. I immediately got excited.

"Sorry to make my patient wait, but I needed to get in uniform, so I could treat you right," she told me. I loved that she liked to roleplay. It made every sexual encounter with her adventurous.

"Now, how can I make you feel better," she asked me as she straddled me. I rubbed from her knees to her toned thighs. Then, I gripped her supple ass cheeks.

"Let me put this dick in you," I commanded her. Her eyes lit up like she was waiting for me to say that for a long time. Her eagerness to please me turned me on more than knowing I could get her mouth and pussy whenever I felt like it.

"Okay. I will allow it, but only if you can be a good little patient and fuck me in my ass when you're done with my pussy," she bargained as she eyed me boldly. I had never tried anal sex before, but at this stage in my life, I was down for trying new things.

"I'm gonna fuck you in your ass so good," I told her. She smiled so wide, her big bright eyes shined with desire. Then, she leaned back, and pushed her skirt up, so I could pull the red and white thong off her. After that, she caressed my dick for a few seconds, lifted up, and slid her wet pussy on it until it disappeared completely.

"Damn Kiandra. Your shit so wet," I whispered to her, before I kissed her luscious lips, and caressed her breasts. I carefully sucked on her erect chestnut brown nipples as she rode me into the sunset. I nibbled on her nipples a bit as she thumbed her clit. After about ten minutes, she came hard on my dick. I wrapped my hands around her waist and assisted her.

"Oh Quincy. I love this dick so much," she moaned as I stirred my dick into her. I sandwiched my small bottom lip between my front teeth while I concentrated on serving her body right.

"You sure you love this dick," I questioned her. She closed her eyes and braced herself for another orgasm. As she came, I bounced her on my dick faster.

"Ooooh shit. I do," she cried out as she orgasmed back-to-back. I stood up with her legs wrapped around my waist, and she rode my dick like it was a pogo stick. I bent my knees and held onto her waist as I plunged into her.

"Shit Kiandra you about to make me nut," I groaned. My legs were getting weak, so I walked back to the couch, and laid her down on it as I stayed inside her. I put one of my knees on the chair and placed my other foot on the floor. Then, I held her legs up and pumped into her until my seed permeated her garden. Raw pussy had become my new weakness, so it was safe to say I wasn't going to carry condoms with me at all times anymore. I hadn't really thought much about whether I was okay with Kiandra giving birth to my babies, but I was just living in the moment with her. Hopefully, I didn't have to think about being a father to her kids any time soon. I wanted to go with the flow and have fun with her. I pulled out of her, and she immediately came out of the position she was in so she could lick our potion off my dick. When she was done, she reached in the drawer of her coffee table, and handed me a bottle of lubricant. Then, she knelt on the armrest of the couch with her legs pressed together and supported the rest of her body by stretching her arm out and placing it on the opposite armrest. She leaned forward and waited for me to enter her from behind. After I slathered the lube on my shaft, I stood behind her with my legs spread a little, and grabbed her ass as I slowly entered her from behind.

"Aw fuck," we both said in unison as I fed her more of me. This was my first time trying anal, so I didn't expect it to feel like it did. It felt weird, but good. Kiandra relaxed her body like a professional. That shit amazed me because I could never. I stroked her slowly because I was afraid, I would hurt her if I went faster.

"Fuck me, Quincy," she demanded.

"You sure?"

"Yeah! I can take it," she assured me. I reluctantly sped up my pace and added some ass smacks in between.

"Yes! Just like that," she praised. I stroked her deeper with each pump. I was still apprehensive about how much dick to give her, but she took whatever I gave her, and I was impressed. I knew she was a freak, but I still became amazed at everything she did that was new to me. I could tell she enjoyed sex on a spiritual level as well as an emotional and physical level. She enthralled herself in each experience, and always outperformed me. I never minded it though because I knew I wasn't on her level. I had just given myself the freedom to not always wear condoms, so I was still just getting started. I shifted into third gear and dicked her down like I knew she wanted. I knew because her body language told me I wasn't satisfying her. I may not have been as adventurous in the bedroom as she was, but I wanted to perform to the best of my ability. She deserved at least that much from me.

"Mmmhm. That's it. Fuck me in my ass just like that, Q," she encouraged me. I smirked because she was giving me the reaction I wanted. I reached around her pelvic bone and stimulated her clit, so she could have a stronger orgasm. Her body tensed up a bit once I started hitting her spot.

"God damn," I grunted as I slid in and out of her lubricated asshole. I didn't know if it was the lube or her natural lubricant, but whatever it was made it more enjoyable to me. I didn't expect to nut off of anal, but I was almost at climax too.

"Aaaah, fuck," Kiandra moaned as she orgasmed. After about four more pumps, I pulled out of her and sprayed my creamy cum on her ass cheeks. I tried not to look at my dick because I would flip the fuck out if I had shit on it. I should have worn a condom to avoid that. Kiandra had a way of making me forget, though. As if she knew what I was thinking, Kiandra rushed to the bathroom to get something to clean me up. She helped me get dressed when she was done cleaning. I loved the way she catered to me like I was her king. I bent down and kissed her on her forehead as I prepared to leave. Before I could walk off, she grabbed my hand and pulled me back.

"Can you please stay just a little while longer," she asked me as she looked at me through puppy dog eyes. I stared at her for a while as I thought about it. I usually left when we were done having sex, but today I was feeling generous.

I looked at my phone and said, "Aight. I'll give you a few more hours of my time." Her eyes lit up like it was the fourth of July. I took my button up shirt back off and laid it across her loveseat. Then, I sat down beside her on her couch. She kissed me like I just made her life.

"Damn. What was that for," I asked her. She mesmerized me with her dark eyes and compelled me with her femininity.

"I'm happy you're here with me. You know, most times you run out of here like you can't wait to get away from me. After what I did to you, I get it. I don't deserve your trust, but I really am sorry. I've wanted nothing but to show you that," she admitted. What she said to me made me feel bad. What that ugly ass therapist said to me came to my mind for some reason. What if I was a narcissist? What if I was incapable of changing who I was because of it? That was something I didn't want to think about.

"I know you are Kiandra. You've done more than enough to prove that to me. It's just me. I'm the one who has shit to work out," I acknowledged. I didn't know what the fuck I was saying. That was so unlike me. I must have been getting soft.

"You're perfectly fine the way you are, Quincy. I would be in love with you regardless," she assured me. I nodded my head at her and kissed her lips. It was crazy how I kept coming across women who were willing to accept me for me as awful as I was, and I found every reason in the book not to fully accept them. Even Jarrah, the most perfect of them all, wasn't enough for me. What did that say about me?

"You hungry? I can cook something for you if you want," Kiandra offered as she tried to stand up. I pulled her into my arms.

"You don't have to do that… or anything else to keep me here, Ki. Relax. Let's just chill here for a while. I'll take you to dinner later on," I told her. The tears gushed from her eyes like a dam had broken. I held her close to me as I stroked her back. I pushed her aside so much it made her emotional that I wanted to stay with her. That told me a lot about me. I needed to get my shit together. Good women were hard to come by, and I had two that loved me unconditionally. I was chasing after Aurora, but she hadn't even shown me what I was seeing from Kiandra. I didn't even know if she loved me. It seemed like I was just an escape from her hard life. I wanted more, and I expressed it every time we got together, yet she would never explicitly tell me she wanted the same. If I was making Kiandra feel like Aurora made me feel after every encounter with her, I needed to get my shit together fast. She may have betrayed me in the beginning, but she did all she could to apologize to me. I knew now that she only did what she did because she felt used by me, so I needed to treat her better than I had been. I hated to admit it, but that therapist was right. I was only interested in fixing myself because I wanted to prove to Jarrah that I could be a better man. However, I still genuinely wanted to become better too. I may have had a challenging time seeing some of my faults, but I never pretended I had it all together. I really wanted to be the man Mama Charmaine saw in me, I just didn't know how.

Chapter 18: Chicago Dreams

March 8, 2017
The Vargas Brothers Architecture Company
Chicago, Illinois

When my plane landed at Chicago O'Hare International Airport, nostalgia overcame me as I looked out the window of my business class seat. I would have never believed it if someone had told me I'd be back in Chicago again. My energy coming here the first time was way different than my energy now. I was in a better headspace since Jarrah wasn't my reason for being here. This was an authentic business trip, and one that I did not want to fuck up. That's why I brought my assistant Janet and Kiandra with me. Since I hired two new managers to help me run my hotels, I was able to take business trips like this with no worries. When Jarrah and I were together, I used to send her to out of town business meetings, so I could stay and watch my hotels. She told me I needed to hire managers back then, but I was too stubborn to listen. I was glad I had grown since then because I was standing in my own way without even knowing it. Thank God for the awakening, even though it came late as hell. I was on the right track to being the man Mama raised me to be. I just needed to reconcile my differences with my brother while I was here. After the conversation we had a few days ago when he came to Atlanta to discuss some urgent family business with me, I was regretful that I didn't try harder to gain his forgiveness. I hoped I would be able to spend time with him while I was in The Windy City so we could try to rehash things. I knew now that it wasn't his fault how things happened, so I shouldn't have held anything against him. We shared in the trauma of our broken family, but we needed to be the ones to break the generational curses. It was the only way I could start my life over with a clean slate.

Once we were cleared to leave the plane, Kiandra, Janet, and I made our way through TSA with no issues. This was just an overnight trip, so we didn't need luggage. I told them to try and pack as light as they could, so we wouldn't be held up at the airport. My appointment with Dario was at nine in the morning, but we couldn't get a flight until after ten. I made sure and informed him that I would be over an hour late since I had late notice, and he was cool with it. When we left out of the airport, there was a car out front waiting for us. I guess this was how The Vargas Brothers treated you when you were a genuine client of theirs. I helped Janet and Kiandra in the backseat before I got in the front with the driver. He took us straight to the twins' office building. Once we arrived, I noticed they had the building secured. Before, you could just walk right in and talk to the receptionist, but they installed metal detectors we had to walk through before getting in the lounge area, and there was security outside and inside. I could tell something was up, but I figured after everything they went through with us, this was the smartest thing to do.

Their assistant, Cynthia, picked up the phone and let Dario know we were there as soon as we walked in. I was actually shocked they were back in business so soon after everything that went down, but when you had the money they had, someone trying to ruin your reputation usually didn't go far. Kiandra, my assistant, and I sat in the lounge area, and waited for them to call us to the back. I watched Kiandra as she scanned the lounge area. I could tell she was amazed by what she saw. Chicago was a different world for her since she had barely been outside of Georgia after her family moved there from Jamaica. I brought her with me because I wanted her to get a glimpse of what I was trying to build for myself. We had been spending a lot of time together ever since we had that breakthrough a few days ago. I hadn't heard from Aurora in a while, so I felt like it would have been stupid of me not to give Kiandra a chance since she genuinely loved me. I loved being around her. She may not have had everything together like Aurora, but she was getting there, which was better than nothing. I respected her for that. Besides, she treated me like I was the best thing that's ever graced the earth in her lifetime, and I was. We men never consider why women reacted to us a certain way. We get so caught up on ego that we missed the important stuff. I was determined to pay attention this time around though.

"Mr. Carter! Mr. Vargas is ready to see you now," Cynthia informed me. Although she was nice, I could tell she didn't care for me like that, and I couldn't blame her. I tried to threaten the twins' livelihood, which meant I was threatening hers. However, I knew it was deeper than that. She was an older woman, so I wouldn't be surprised if she saw them as her family. That was more than enough to garner her dislike. I couldn't say I cared though. As long as the twins were cool enough to do business with me, I couldn't care less what anyone else thought. Janet and I stood up to go to the back, but Kiandra remained seated. When I realized she wasn't behind me, I looked back, and reached my hand out for her to come with us. She stared at my hand for a while as if she couldn't believe I wanted her to come in the meeting with me. Then, she got up and followed me.

I wrapped my arm around her waist, and whispered, "I need you by my side." She didn't react, but I could tell it was because she was trying to keep her emotions in check, so I left her alone. Dario's door was open, but I still knocked before I entered.

"You can come in," he told me. I hesitantly walked in when I saw Deandra's husband in there with him. He stared at me hard like we had beef. I hoped and prayed he didn't know I was fucking her while he was in prison. I didn't want any problems with him. Shit, I was afraid of the twins, and I knew they had nothing on him. I tried to avoid eye contact with him because I felt like he would see through me. I didn't have the best poker face when it came to men. Women were a bit easier to fool.

"What's up Q? Good morning, ladies," Dario greeted the three of us as we stood before him.

"Good morning," Kiandra responded in a low tone. I needed to take her out more often so she could be used to being around these types of people. You could look at her and tell she was out of her element. Hell, she was wearing a mini dress to a meeting. I guess she felt like because she threw a blazer over it, it was business meeting appropriate. That's my fault though. I should have taken her shopping before we came, but I didn't have time to.

"Morning," Janet replied with her nose in the sky like she was stuck up. I hoped she didn't talk out of turn so she wouldn't mess this up for me. She came from money, so she wasn't impressed by Dario's office. Regardless of her background, though, she was an assistant, so she needed to chill out.

"Y'all can have a seat," Dario told us as he pointed to the three chairs in front of his.

"No y'all can't. Not until y'all introduce yourselves," Jerrell chimed in as he stared at Kiandra like she was filet mignon on a golden platter. Dario chuckled at him. The way he looked at her made me a little jealous. I had become territorial over her in the brief time we spent together.

"He's just kidding around. Don't pay him any mind," Dario directed toward the ladies as the three of us sat down.

"Dario, this is my assistant, Janet," I introduced as Dario eyed Janet. Janet was five feet and ten inches tall with beautiful long light-yellow brown legs. She looked like she was white, but she was mixed with African American and Cuban. She had long straight red hair and her round face was almost fully covered in freckles. She was full figured, but not a BBW. She had light green eyes, a cute dainty nose, and full pink lips that gave her ethnicity away. I hired her because I wasn't attracted to white or in her case, white passing women, so I could trust myself not to touch her. Plus, she was married, and very loyal to her husband, who was a college friend of mine. She needed a job after being a stay-at-home mother for a few years, so I hired her as my assistant as a favor to her husband. Dario held his hand out for her to shake it, but when she offered him hers, he kissed the back of it. I rolled my eyes internally as Janet blushed at him.

"This is Kiandra. My… girlfriend," I announced. Kiandra and Janet jerked their heads toward me abruptly. I hadn't meant for it to come out like that, but I think the man in me wanted to make it clear that she was off limits.

"Girlfriend," Dario questioned as he squinted his eye at me and flipped his lip up in disbelief. Both Janet and Kiandra flashed owl-like eyes at me as shock consumed them.

"Damn, even she can't believe that shit," Jerrell remarked. Dario laughed at him. I knew they both could see through me, but I didn't care. They took Jarrah away from me, and I was damned if I let that shit happen again. Dario held his hand out to shake Kiandra's hand, but before he could try anything, she clasped his hand into hers and shook it, which boosted my ego a bit. I knew she was loyal though, so I wasn't worried about her. I did want to make it known she was mine though. It was easy to be charmed by Dario and Dustin. Deandra's husband wasn't charming, but women were usually drawn to men like him because he made them feel secure since he had that no-nonsense, bad boy persona.

"She's a real one, Q. You should keep her around," Dario suggested as his gaze caressed Kiandra like he couldn't help himself. She was beautiful as hell, so I wasn't shocked they were drooling over her like they were. I didn't need him telling me that for me to realize it. I only brought Kiandra and Janet with me because I knew they would help set the tone of the meeting. Even Dario and Dustin couldn't deny a beautiful woman when they saw one, and I knew they'd be on their best behavior in front of them. However, I didn't expect Jerrell to be around, which made me feel like something was up.

"Where's Dustin," I asked Dario. Jerrell and his glance dipped to each other and then they turned their attention back to me.

"Dustin's at home with the ladies. Don't worry, though. He got his crew together to get your hotel finished. We just need you to sign the new contracts first," he explained. I nodded my head. If Dustin was with Jarrah, then someone must have been coming after them again.

"Is everything okay? I noticed the security in the front."

"Yeah, everything is-"

"Nah. My wife's pussy caused some trouble for us, so we're looking for the muthafuckas that shot at us a few days ago. You know, yo boy. That dirty ass Mexican nigga. You wouldn't know nothin' about that, right," Jerrell questioned, interrupting Dario. My heart raced as he mean-mugged me. I wasn't surprised to hear that Donald was still after them, but

I was surprised he casually admitted Deandra fucked Donald. That alarmed me because only she could have told him that.

"No. After y'all left Atlanta, I paid him half a mill to leave me out of his bullshit. I haven't seen him since," I explained in a calm tone. Jerrell stared at me for a few seconds as he processed what I said.

"J, this ain't the time or place for that shit. Go find you something to do 'cause you been on one since they got here," Dario chimed in before Jerrell could respond. I was glad he said something because Jerrell was making all of us uncomfortable.

"I am doing something. Think of me as your personal bodyguard 'cause I don't trust this nigga," Jerrell responded as he patted the gun tucked in his jeans. It was crazy to me how different these niggas were. When I was rampaging, I never even stopped to consider who I was up against, but I was way out of my league. It took me being on the other side of things to realize it, but I'm glad I was able to be on the other side of it because I was digging my grave for them to put me in when I was in the warzone.

"Jerrell, chill the fuck out. You makin' me have to use my hood voice in front of these beautiful ladies and shit," Dario said as he looked back and forth between Kiandra and Janet. You'd think he was single the way he was flirting with them. I couldn't talk though. I wasn't faithful by a long shot.

"Aight, but only if I can take them with me," Jerrell stated. I frowned.

"I'm a married woman," Janet interjected as she flashed her ring. She responded before I could say anything.

"So. I'm a married man, but I don't give a fuck about them vows. I'm married, not monogamous. Besides, I'm not tryna to take y'all from this country ass nigga. I'm gonna show y'all around while these two boring ass niggas talk business," Jerrell countered. I looked at Dario for confirmation.

"They good with him. He ain't as hard as he try to pretend he is," Dario assured me. I nodded my head at Kiandra and Janet to give them my answer. Janet jumped up like she was eager, but Kiandra was hesitant to go with him.

"Come on, shorty. You aight with me. I don't want this nigga's sloppy seconds, unless-"

"I'll put a bullet through your head if you even think about it," Dario barked before he could finish his sentence. Even the idea of him mentioning Jarrah's name brought out the killer in Dario. Jerrell chuckled as he left the room in front of Kiandra and Janet.

Kiandra looked back at me before she walked out of the office. I knew she didn't want to leave my side, but I did need privacy to talk business with Dario. I'd make it up to her once we were done though.

"Looks like she's in love with you," Dario said to me once we were alone. I fought hard to control my cheek muscles as they tried to expose the way I felt.

"Yeah, it seems that way," I responded dryly. He smirked.

"You know, I ain't expected you to move on so soon. Thought I'd have to fight you a little more before that happened," he teased. I chuckled.

"Well, I had to move on at some point."

"I guess that's true. I damn sure wasn't giving her back," he remarked. I shook my head at him. Jarrah definitely had him drinking the same Kool-Aid that got me hooked. I couldn't blame him though.

"How is she?"

"She's as good as she can be. The baby's been kicking her ass though," he told me.

"Let her know I asked about her," I replied. He scowled at me.

"You not gone go see her," he inquired. I'm sure he was shocked I said that since I would have never missed an opportunity to see Jarrah, but I needed to let her go so I could move on.

"Damn. You serious about that shit I see," Dario said. I held eye contact with him to show him that I was serious.

"I respect that… Anyways, let's get to this business," he told me as he slid the contract in front of me. I didn't even bother to read it. I knew I could trust them because I could trust Jarrah. Plus, I was in no position to be difficult with them after what I did.

"You sure you don't need a lawyer to look at it," Dario inquired as I signed the contract.

"I'm sure that as long as you love her, I got nothing to worry about," I told him as I kept my attention on the contract. He chuckled. He knew as well as I did that Jarrah would never let them betray me, and I had a feeling that even without her influence, they wouldn't have. I realized they weren't bad people. It was me who made them act out of character.

"Aight then. Just so you know, Dustin doubled his price for his troubles," he told me. I pulled out the check I had already written for them before I even came to Chicago and handed it to him. He snickered as he looked at it.

"You sure you wanna give us half a mill? The asking price is just-"

"I'm sure," I told him in a stern tone. He stared at me for a while.

"Okay. I'm never gonna complain about extra money... I guess everything is squared away. Your hotel is finished by the way. I was just bullshitting earlier," he admitted to me. My eyes lit up.

"Really?"

"Yeah. It was almost done before you pulled that lawsuit shit on us. I just didn't tell you because you were trippin'," Dario elaborated.

"How though? It had been only a few weeks since you started," I said. He smiled.

"Yeah. My brother is a genius. You think we got all this money by luck? We got a gift. Regardless of if we were present or not, this company damn near runs on its own. That's why I can come and go as I please."

"Damn. I was really no match for the two of you," I unintentionally admitted. Dario laughed.

"You damn sure weren't, but if you play your cards right, you could attain at least a quarter of our greatness."

"You offering to help me," I questioned. He stared at me for a while as he thought about it.

"Only for you to pay Jarrah back that money she gave you. Not because she needs it, but because you know she deserves it," he told me. I eyed his desk briefly at the mention of that since I'd been wanting to do that as soon as I could.

"You're right. That's all I've been wanting to do, but I knew what I had wasn't enough. If you help me, I promise I will give her every dime I owe her," I vowed. He bowed his head at me.

"Okay, cool. Now, let me take you to see your hotel," he smiled as he stood up. He grabbed the contract I just signed and the check for half a million and walked around his desk. I stood up and followed him. I couldn't believe my hotel was done this whole time. If I had known, I would have surrendered earlier than I did. Having a hotel in Chicago was sentimental to me for more reasons than one. The most important one, though, was to honor my father's wishes. Before we got outside, Dario handed the contract and check to his assistant. The way they trusted her proved I was right about her being their family. I needed to build an environment like that for my businesses, so I could have people around me that wanted me to win as much as their employees did. If I could follow their business model, I'd be huge.

Chapter 19: The Carter IV

March 8, 2015
The Carter IV
Chicago, Illinois

Everything left my mind as we rode through downtown Chicago. I may not have been a fan of the twins because of Jarrah, but I admired Dustin's work, so I couldn't wait to see what he created for me. I couldn't believe he finished my hotel so quickly. It made me feel even more like an asshole because of how I acted toward them when they did nothing to me. What I had going on with Jarrah had nothing to do with them, but I made it their issue. I was definitely trying to make up for the trouble I caused. That's why I wrote that check for five hundred thousand dollars. I knew what they did for me was worth more than anything I could give them. Not only did they decide to give me my hotel, but they had given me a pass for all the trouble I caused even though they were still dealing with the aftermath. Jarrah may have influenced their decision, but I knew they were also being nice to me. Dario didn't have to help me with my business, but the fact that he offered showed me what type of man he was. He wasn't proud, greedy, and power hungry like I was. They were just successful black men that worked hard as hell for what they had. I should have respected that enough not to go after their business.

I looked out of my window as I thought of how far I had come. When I was a little boy, I dreamed of owning a business in the city where my father was born. That dream was solidified when I received a sketch of skyscrapers that was sent to me when I was in college. I wasn't sure who sent the sketch, but I had an idea. I may not have known much about my father, but I still had the desire to make him proud even though he was no longer here. If I had known I would get to see my hotel today, I would have brought my mother with me so she could witness it with me. This was a huge moment. Not only for me, but for my whole family. I was a first-generation millionaire, and that meant a whole lot coming from Atlanta. I took a deep breath as I prepared myself for this moment. I hadn't laid eyes on my hotel while they were building it, so I was going into this completely blind. I remembered how I felt when I picked out the land, I wanted it built on. It was surreal to me because when I first came to Chicago, I only got in business with the twins, so I could learn my enemy after my private investigator told me Jarrah was seeing one of them. Building my hotel wasn't even my plan, but I figured I would have killed two birds with one stone since I had access to the best architect duo in the country. However, I thought my dream was lost because of my foolishness, so it was bizarre it was still coming true.

When Dario made a right on South Michigan Avenue, I prepared myself to be blown away. I kept my eyes on the street as we slowly approached the area that was once a plot of land. My mouth dropped as I laid eyes on The Carter IV. It was twenty-four floors of pure beauty. The three hundred and eighty-four foot of curved, cool blue glass that was reminiscent to the Michigan River mesmerized me immediately. I marveled at it as Dario parked in the parking lot that was on the right side of the building. There was also an underground parking garage with an entrance at the back of it. We quietly got out of his Porsche and walked to the front of the building. When I was standing in front of it, I stopped to see it from a different angle, and it was gorgeous from all sides. Dario waited for me before he walked inside. I stood in front of the front door for a while as I took everything in. I knew the outside of the hotel had nothing on the inside, so I knew I was in for a treat.

"You might want to pull yourself together before you walk inside," Dario warned me, drawing my attention to the tears on my cheeks. I hadn't even realize I was crying. I was just so full of pride and happiness that I couldn't help myself. I dried my eyes, and slowly waved my hand on the sensor to open the door. As the doors opened, my eyes connected with Jarrah's gorgeous hazel eyes.

"Surprise," everyone yelled as I walked through the door. I scanned the room, and laid eyes on Jarrah, Terry, Kiandra, Janet, Jerrell, and Jarrah's mother-in-law. I was so surprised they did this for me after all the problems I caused. I knew I had Jarrah and Terry to thank for this, but I was still grateful. I slowly turned back toward Dario and stared at him. He smirked and shrugged his shoulders.

"Don't look at me. You know who's responsible," Dario said. I turned my attention to Jarrah who was cheesing at me. I started over to her as I kept my eyes locked on hers.

"I know that pussy special, but I don't know if I got it in me to do no shit like this. I wish Deandra would ask me some shit like this," I heard Jerrell say as I made my way toward Jarrah.

"Nigga shut the fuck up. You talk too damn much... and don't ever say shit else about my girl's pussy to me... or anybody else," Dario spat. I laughed internally at the two of them as I stayed in the moment like I was the star in a cheesy movie about love. It was like Jarrah and I was in slow motion while everyone else moved at normal speed. Before I could reach Jarrah, Kiandra ran toward me at full speed and jumped into my arms. She threw her arms around my neck and kissed me like she was about to suck my dick next. I pulled away from her and put her down on her feet. She hugged me again before I could push her to the side. I peeked over her shoulder and stared at Jarrah. I was annoyed that Kiandra's actions wiped the smile off her face.

"I'm so happy for you, Quincy," Kiandra told me as she stared into my eyes. I smiled at her and kissed her forehead before I brushed past her, and stood in front of Jarrah, who was about six feet away from us. I wanted to avoid her on this trip, but fate was against that. I knew seeing her would set my progress back with Kiandra and Aurora, and it scared me. I knew the only way I was going to move on was if I cut our contact to just the phone. I didn't see this surprise coming at all, and I had to admit that I was shocked the twins allowed it. It made sense why Dario was adamant about me paying her back after he had assured me, she didn't need my chump change. I knew Jarrah was special, but with everything she pulled off as far as they were concerned, she became more special to me. We stood in front of each other and gazed into the stars in our eyes. Jarrah reached out and hugged me.

"I'm so proud of you, Quincy," she said in my ear as she rested her chin on my shoulder.

"Thank you! I know this wouldn't have happened if it weren't for you," I told her as I squeezed her tight. Without her influence Dario and Dustin would never have told me my hotel was ready for business, and I couldn't blame them because I honestly didn't deserve to have it.

"Damn, when I'm gonna get a turn," Theresa interjected as she stood beside us and mean-mugged us for leaving her out. I reached my arm out for her, and pulled her into me, so we could do a group hug.

"Awww," Jarrah sang as she wrapped her arm around Theresa's waist. Then, the three of us got quiet for a while as we loved each other.

"I know Mama is smiling so hard right now," Theresa said, disrupting our moment of silence. We got quiet again as we soaked the moment in. Mama Charmaine always encouraged me to go after my dreams, no matter how ambitious I would get. I knew she was proud I had finally gotten my hotel chain to Chicago, the city of my roots. I could picture her right now, her smile iridescent like the sunlight. *Quincy, my boy, you did it like I knew you would,* I heard in her voice. The tears started trickling down my face uncontrollably, and it must have been contagious because I could feel Jarrah and Theresa's tears fall on my shoulders. After a while, the three of us separated, and I swiped the tears from both of their eyes. Jarrah swiped the tears from my right eye, and Terry dried my left eye. Kiandra immediately came to console me.

"I'm okay," I assured her as she cupped my cheek in her hand. She nodded at me.

"Jarrah, Terry, this is Kiandra… my girlfriend," I introduced. Jarrah and Theresa looked at me like I had lost my mind, so I knew what was coming.

"Your what," Jarrah questioned as she scowled at me. I could hear Dario and Jerrell laughing behind me.

"Kiandra? Ain't that the bitch that falsely accused you of raping her or something," Theresa asked. Kiandra stepped behind me like she was afraid they would hit her. I hadn't filled them in on what was going on, so they didn't know she was back in the picture.

"It was sexual harassment actually, but she apologized for what she did, and we worked things out," I explained.

"You mean she fucked you and deep throated your little dick, and you just forgot that she was the enemy. Uhm, uhm, uhm… I thought your ass was changing for real," Theresa responded. Jarrah giggled at her.

"Honestly, Q, I'm happy you moved on. At this point, I'll take anything other than what you were doing before this," Jarrah stated. I rolled my eyes at her for setting her expectations for me as low as she had.

"What happened to the bitch with the husband," Theresa questioned. I bucked my eyes at her for disclosing that information. I kept my dealings with Aurora a secret from Kiandra. Jarrah smacked Theresa on the arm when she realized she was snitching on me.

"Ouch! Why would you do that? You know you heavy handed as hell," she told Jarrah. Then, she turned her attention to Kiandra, who was giving me a death stared that scared me a little.

"Whoops," Theresa sarcastically remarked. I knew she knew what she was doing.

"Aurora is out of the picture for good. Kiandra is my girl," I finally responded as I stared into Kiandra's eyes to make sure she understood me. She exhaled deeply and flashed me a faint smile. Then, she stepped forward, and held her hand out for Jarrah and Theresa to shake.

"Hi! Nice to officially meet you two. I've heard a lot about you," she said as she shook Jarrah's hand. Jarrah eyed me like she was trying to put two and two together. I had been dealing with Kiandra before I decided to divorce Jarrah, but we hadn't had sex since she had an issue with me being married. Kiandra was my assistant, so they never dealt with each other directly, but Jarrah knew how long she had been working for me.

"Nice to meet you too," Jarrah said, deciding not to share her thoughts. I was happy she played it cool. I definitely didn't want any drama right now. Once Jarrah let Kiandra's hand go Kiandra extended her hand to Theresa, but Theresa crossed her arms over each other, refusing to shake Kiandra's hand. I could tell Kiandra was disappointed because she dropped her hand like someone threw an anchor in it. I grabbed her hand and stroked her soft skin with my fingers to ease her mind.

"Congratulations, Mr. Carter," Janet interjected as we stood in awkward silence. Then, she gave me a church hug.

"Thank you, Janet," I told her through a smile.

"Where's Dustin? I wanted to thank him for doing this for me," I said as I turned my attention to Dario.

"He's at his house with Deandra," Dario responded. I frowned.

"By himself?"

"Yeah. Why you asked that," Jerrell questioned. I could have kicked myself for saying that aloud. I had forgotten he was here with us. He studied my body language as I tried to figure out how to respond.

"Alright, why don't I take everyone on a tour of the hotel since Dustin isn't here to do it," Dario announced, saving my ass for the second time. I was so stupid I almost exposed Deandra and myself. When we were together, she talked about her feelings for Dustin, and she told me a secret I never wanted to repeat or know for that matter. Jerrell was crazy, so I couldn't imagine how he'd react to the shit his wife was hiding.

"I'll have to take a rain check. My man is getting his ankle monitor taken off today, so I gotta go. We'll come to Dustin's house when we're done," Theresa stated. Everyone except her prepared to follow Dario on a tour of the hotel. I was excited to see everything for the first time. As Dario escorted us through The Carter IV, I gaped at the urban modern interior design. Although I had to furnish it myself, Dustin had some of his famous handmade furniture in various parts of the hotel. My favorite of his signature pieces were the handmade oakwood three-legged end tables in the lounge area, and the oakwood geometric receptionist's desk in the lobby. I also loved the rose gold raceway art deco-style wallpaper that was placed on certain walls in the hotel. It gave the minimalistic designs just enough flavor to tie in the whole look and feel. I was glad to see that Dustin outdid himself on my hotel. It was obvious that he loved what he did. He was a true artist, and I was glad to say I owned a hotel that was built by Dustin Vargas.

Chapter 20: Be Careful What You Wish For

March 16, 2017
Highland Square Apartment Complex
Atlanta, Georgia

After being in Chicago for a week and a half getting The Carter IV prepared for the grand opening, I was happy to be back in Atlanta. I loved owning a business in Chicago, but the city just wasn't for me. However, I knew it only made sense for me to buy a condo for when I needed to be there for business and to spend time with Jarrah, Terry, and Marcus. I met up with my brother when I had some free time. We had our own family drama we were dealing with, and my old acquaintance was at the center of it. However, Marcus informed me that he hadn't heard from Donald since he showed up at his job and threatened him. I guess I was right that he wasn't anything for us to worry about. Besides, he was more concerned with getting revenge for his sister's murder still. Dario filled me in on the drama they had been going through with Donald because of Deandra. They were all staying at Dustin's house to keep each other safe, so I couldn't see Jarrah after they surprised me at my hotel. Although Donald's attention was more so on Dario, Deandra, and her husband, I still hated that

Jarrah was caught in it by default. However, I had to trust the twins to take care of her. She was their problem now. I had one of my own to focus on. I pulled Kiandra into me as I breathed in her fresh scent. Being beside her made me feel complete. I kissed her on her shoulder as she slept in my arms. It was crazy to me how I was pushing her away from me a while ago, and now I always wanted her near me.

A few days ago, Kiandra got sick while we were in Chicago. She had been throwing everything up she ate. At first, we thought it was a stomach bug, until it got so bad, we had to take her to the emergency room. That is where we found out we were going to have a baby. I was so happy I was finally going to be a father. Just a few weeks ago, I didn't think I wanted kids with her, but that was before I realized I was in love with her. I think I had known all along. That's why I kept her at a distance. She terrified me because she loved me so fiercely, and I hadn't wanted that from any woman other than Jarrah. Moving on from her was difficult for me because I knew what I was losing by losing her. However, it may have been the best thing that happened to me considering everything I gained from it.

Jarrah and I were still in each other's lives, so technically I didn't lose her. I just had to let go of that perfect image I held of her because that wasn't who Jarrah was at all. The person she was when she was with the twins was the person she was. It took me being around Dario to realize it. The way I loved her had nothing on the way they loved her. I could never allow her to be free enough to love all the people who needed her. That's how I knew we weren't made for each other. This beautiful dark sable-skinned queen lying beside me was my soulmate. She proved it to me every day. I learned so much about Kiandra once I started looking deeper than her surface. She was smart as hell, and she trusted me enough to submit to me. That meant more to me than anything. After we spent so much time together, she told me about the dreams she had for herself, and I was amazed by it. Turns out, she was going to school to become a sports medicine doctor. She only had one more year left in school. I knew she was into fitness and physical health, but I had no idea she was pursuing sports medicine as a career. She amazed me. I kissed her back, and she squirmed in my arms. I knew I was getting on her nerves since she hadn't been able to sleep much, but I couldn't help myself.

"Ki, it's time to wake up," I gently whispered in her ear. She raised her shoulder and brushed it across her ear. I chuckled as I watched her be annoyed by me.

"Kiandra, we have to get ready for today," I pushed.

"Quincy please… I'm so tired," she whined as she flipped over on her left side to face me. I kissed her lips when they were close to mine, and she smiled.

"Unless you greet me with that morning wood, I suggest you give me my space," she told me. I chuckled. As if she wasn't freaky enough, dick was all that was on her mind these days. Who was I kidding? That had been the way she was since the day I met her.

"You know you don't feel well enough to do any of that. Besides, we got things to do today. Remember," I asked her. She sat up sluggishly and leaned against the larch wood and rubber wood headboard that had channel tufted upholstery.

"Okay. Okay, I'm getting up," she pouted. I kissed her lips, and then her forehead. Then, I got up to take a piss, and get the shower ready for us. I brushed my teeth and washed my face as I waited for Kiandra to join me in the bathroom. As soon as she walked through the door, the vomit was coming up. She ran to the toilet and the puke came out of her like she had an exorcism performed on her. I had a weak stomach, so I flushed the toilet as soon as I got to her. I rubbed her back as she hunched over the toilet on her knees.

"You okay baby," I asked her. She nodded her head at me. I kissed the top of her head before I walked off to get her some napkins to wipe her mouth. Then, I sat the stool in front of her side of the vanity, so she could brush her teeth and clean her face. When she was done, I picked her up and sat her on the shower chair in the shower. I stepped in the shower, grabbed our washcloths, and sat on the other end of the shower chair, so I could wash her off. After I was done with her upper body, I worked on her lower body. I learned how to clean a woman's vagina from Jarrah, so I did all of that for her. Although I hated that she was going through this, I loved taking care of her like this. It made me appreciate her body a lot more than I did in the past. I knew this was hard for her, and I could tell she was putting on a brave face for me. I didn't need to hear her say it to know that having my baby this soon wasn't in her plans. Kiandra wanted kids as much as I did, but I knew she wanted to finish school first. I understood that, and I appreciated her for deciding to have my baby, even though it didn't happen in the order neither of us wanted it to be in.

"Q," she called as I washed her feet.

"Yeah," I asked her as I focused on cleaning between her toes.

"Thank you," she responded. I looked into her eyes that were blurry with tears.

"For what," I asked her as I thumbed a tear away.

"For loving me back. You don't know how long I've been waiting for you to love me back, and I'm just so-" she was about to say, but her tears muted her words. I wrapped my arms around her and kissed her forehead. I felt bad that it took me so long to realize I had gold in front of me the whole time I was looking for diamonds.

"I'm sorry Ki. I'm sorry it took me so long to recognize I had all I needed in you. I was stupid, but I promise I will make you the happiest woman alive every day for the rest of our lives," I vowed before I kissed her sweet lips. She slowly stood up and straddled me as she kept her lips entwined in mine.

"Ki, are you sure about this? I don't want to make you sick," I told her as she stroked my half hard dick, turning it into steel like she was a shape shifter.

"Don't deny me of what's mine, Q. Besides, this is the only thing that doesn't make me sick," she replied. I smirked as she slid my dick inside her. It felt like she had tucked my shit into bed. I sucked the small puddle of water that was in the dent next to her collar bone, making her exhale deeply. She whined her hips as she slowly bounced up and down. I flicked my tongue across her sensitive nipples, making her shudder.

"Aaaah," Kiandra moaned as she coated my dick with her nectar. I grabbed her by the waist and pumped into her deeper and faster, making her cream on my shaft again.

“Mmm Quincy. More. I want more,” she cried out as I kept that rhythm, giving her what she was asking for. I sucked on her juicy, firm breasts as she rode me.

“That’s right baby. Cum on Daddy’s dick,” I praised as she released again. The timing of her orgasms was boosting my ego, so I went harder. I held her toned thick thighs in my hands as I bounced her on me. She dug into my back and shoulder with her dull nails. I was glad she was in between sets because I was still wearing scratches from those acrylics she liked to wear sometimes.

“Aw fuck,” we both said as we orgasmed together. Kiandra loosened her grip on my neck as she sucked on my bottom lip. I stroked her stomach with my fingers.

“Thank you for carrying my baby. I know the timing isn’t ideal, but I appreciate you for making my dreams come true,” I confessed to Kiandra. She grinned and pecked my lips.

“I love you, Quincy. Having your baby and creating a legacy with you is an honor.”

“Even though Mama’s boo boo has been giving her a hard time, Mama still loves her very much,” she said in the tone people used when they talked to babies. I playfully rolled my eyes at her for using that irritating voice.

"Her? I like the sound of that," I responded. I always dreamed of having a little girl, so I would be excited if my dreams came true. I couldn't wait to spoil my little princess or prince. I wouldn't be mad either way even though I wanted a daughter.

"Let's finish up in here so we can get out of here at a reasonable time. It's going to be hard to get Monalisa out the house, so we need extra time for that," I reminded Kiandra. Then, I kissed her temple, cheeks, nose, and lips while she smiled at me. It was safe to say I was in love. I may not have seen it coming, but my eyes were wide open now, and I was happy with what I was witnessing.

Kiandra and I finished showering, and got dressed, so we could handle the important business we planned to take care of today. Once Ki was ready, I escorted her to the living room, and fixed her a quick fruit salad since that seemed to be the only thing she could keep down. I wasn't trying to clean up vomit again, so I gave her a cold bottle of water to wash it down. For some reason, the room temperature water made her nauseous too. None of it made sense to me, but I was going to do what I could to lessen her suffering. Our baby had been a handful already. I knew I needed to prepare myself for the wild ride fatherhood would be. After Ki was settled, I went to my mother's room door, and knocked on it. This time, she answered it quickly like she had been waiting on me to come check on her. She must have been in a good mood because she greeted me with a smile.

When we told her she was going to be a grandmother, she was happy about it. We still had a lot of work to do on our relationship, but we were going in the right direction. The surprise I had for Monalisa was going to make things even better. Although Dr. McFarlane came at me sideways in my first therapy session, I took in a lot of what he said, and I even went as far as taking some advice from him. It was still hard for me to accept that I was a narcissist, but I was open to the possibility. I didn't want to repeat the same mistakes my parents did, so it was important for me to become a better man. That's why I called to set an appointment for myself before we came back to Atlanta. I'm sure Dr. McFarlane knew things would happen that way, and I was willing to bet he approached me the way he did because he could tell it was the only way to get through to me. I shook my head at the thought of him plotting on me. I gave my mother a hug and kissed her on her forehead. I tried to be as affectionate to her as I could without making her uncomfortable. I knew she wasn't used to me being so warm to her, but I really wanted her to believe I was trying to change into a better son for her.

After the visit we got from Marcus about two weeks ago, she was in better spirits. I was glad my brother finally came around and forgave our mother because it was what she needed to take initiative in her healing. I was still working on earning his forgiveness, but I knew we'd get there some day. With the amount of shit, he dropped on me when he was in Atlanta, it was miraculous that our family was coming together. I still couldn't believe our father was alive this whole time. I always knew he was since I remembered every moment I spent with him as a kid, but knowing for sure made it realer. I didn't know how he hid for thirty years, but I had already tried everything I knew to lure him out. It sucked that Marcus was who he chose to reveal himself to after all those years of me waiting for him to come back. He still hadn't visited me yet. I figured he was keeping his distance so he wouldn't upset Monalisa, so I came up with a plan that might finally lure him out of hiding, even if it were just to reunite with me. Having my mother around had become a routine I was getting used to, but I felt like it was time for a change that would benefit our family. That's why it was important for me to get her out of the house today.

"Good morning, Ma. Are you feeling aight," I asked her as I studied her oval face. I was happy to see a glimmer of hope in her dark brown eyes now. It was a lot better than the sad eyes and tattooed frown and tears she usually wore. I guess reconciling with Marcus and me was something she really needed to want to live again.

"Yeah, I'm good Q. Where's my beautiful daughter in law," she asked me as she brushed past me to get to Kiandra. I shook my head and rolled my eyes at the disrespect. I was a little jealous, but I was happy my mother loved Kiandra. I followed her to the living room as she hurried over to Ki. She hugged her and sat down beside her.

"Good morning, Ki. How are you feeling today," she asked Kiandra. Kiandra sighed.

"Still having a hard time hunh?"

"Yes ma'am. Your son has been taking care of me though," Kiandra replied as she looked at me. I winked at her and made her show all of her pretty white teeth.

"You know we can rub some peppermint oil on your stomach to help it settle, and you can drink some ginger ale too," Monalisa advised. Kiandra nodded her head at her.

"Quincy, take me to the store so I can get some things for my daughter in law to make her feel better," my mother demanded. I shook my head.

"We can stop by the store when we get ready to come back here. There's something we want to show you," I told her. She stared at me like she was confused.

"Something for me," she asked as she pointed to herself.

"Yes Ma. So, come on. Let's go," I rushed them. We had a meeting that would start in twenty minutes, and it was going to take at least fifteen minutes for us to get where we were going. I went to the refrigerator and got a few bottles of water and stored them in a cooler bag for when Kiandra needed something to soothe her stomach. After that, I made my way to the door, and waited for the two women. Kiandra and Monalisa slowly came to the front door. Before I could twist the knob, I heard a knock on the door. It took me by surprise because I wasn't expecting anyone. I slowly opened the door, and almost shitted myself when I saw her face.

"Aurora," I said as I stared at her. She was in tears as she looked back at me. It shocked and angered me to see the bruises around her eyes, mouth, and nose. She looked like she had been getting abused over time because some of her wounds looked old and some looked fresh. Her left eye was almost swollen shut and dried blood was under her nostril and on the corner of her mouth. If I hadn't seen the long dark wavy hair, and the piercing deep brown eyes, I wouldn't have believed it was her. She stepped across the doorway and hugged my neck like she was in danger, and I was her savior.

"Aurora, what are you doing here? What happened to you? Are you okay," I asked her all at once after pulling away from her. She eyed her feet as she sobbed.

"Quincy… I'm… I'm pregnant and my husband isn't the father," she confessed. My jaw dropped as I processed the information, she gave me. I couldn't believe this was happening to me. My life was finally getting on track, and I was happy with Kiandra. My business was doing well, and I was even in a better space with my mother, my brother, Terry, and Jarrah. Shit, even the twins had become cool with me. I had everything I had been searching for, and it was all going to crumble with the atomic bomb that Aurora just dropped on me. I knew I had to prepare myself for what was going to come of this. The bruises on Aurora's face told me what kind of man her husband was, so I knew I would have to deal with him as well. My obsession with being a parent was going to cost me a lot. Suddenly, I heard Mama Charmaine's voice in my head. *Be careful what you ask for Q. You just might get it.*

To Be Continued…

Black Irish Rose*, book 7 of the Two Monogamous series and part 2 of The Carter Brother's story is coming in October.*

About the Author

S. R. Graham was born in October 1990 in South Carolina, where she still lives. She has a bachelor's degree in creative writing and English attained at Southern New Hampshire University. She is a versatile writer, creating anything from poetry to screenplays. She is the author of the Two Monogamous series and sub-series. S. R. Graham also writes poetry and original screenplays. She has been a published author since 2014, with her first poetry collection, Journey to Love, being her first published book. Currently, she is still writing the Two Monogamous series, poetry collections, the Pretty Privilege series, and the new Robinhood series, amongst other creative projects she's working on. You can purchase a signed copy of her books on her website at srgraham.org. Subscribe to her mailing list on her website so you can be updated about her future work and other news. If you want live updates for her works in progress, join her Facebook group at S. R. Graham's Sensual Beings Group

Thank You: Closing Words

Dear supporter,

Now that you've reached the end of this book, I'd like to thank you for purchasing a copy of *After the Hurricane,* book 6 of my *Two Monogamous* series, and taking the time out to read it. To fill in the gaps of The Carter Brothers' three-part story, stay tuned for Black Irish Rose, coming in October.

As a last request, could you kindly leave an honest review on Amazon, Goodreads, Barnes & Nobles, or whichever bookstore you purchased it from. If you already have a Goodreads account and it's linked to your Amazon account, it will automatically post your Amazon review to your Goodreads account. Writing a few sentences will work fine.

Also, add me on social media for more writing, other projects, and news.

Instagram: thesensualgenius
Twitter: dasensualgenius
Facebook: lovesrgraham
Facebook Book Group: S. R. Graham's Sensual Beings Group
Goodreads: srgrahamwrites
Website: srgraham.org

YouTube: The Sensual Genius

If you want to support, my clothing line visit cellmatesapparel.com

Don't be afraid to reach out to me to discuss my writing. I love getting feedback from my readers. I will personally read and respond to each message I get. Again, thank you for your support! I hope you enjoyed my writing.

Made in the USA
Columbia, SC
23 October 2023

24552381R00141